Douglas Hynden

RAPTURE BEGINS

SCRIPTOR HOUSE
THE EPITOME OF GREATNESS

Scriptor House LLC

2810 N Church St Wilmington, Delaware, 19802

www.scriptorhouse.com

Phone: +1302-205-2043

Published by Scriptor House LLC

Paperback ISBN: 979-8-88692-162-5

eBook ISBN: 979-8-88692-163-2

We are guided through life from birth to death by the values instilled in us by our parents, families, and (in my case) the church too. Some values good and some bad, but always conscious or unconscious decisions to teach those values. I was born in 1952 to parents who loved and nurtured me. There were five children. I was the second child and very quiet until I got into school. I was born David Riley Hunter in a small town in southern Iowa, where everyone knew everybody.

My father was in insurance and real estate with his father, and both worked for our church in their spare time. Through the years, my father dedicated more and more time to our church, and it seemed we were going here and there with him to preach or meet people who were lost and needed a hand to get back on the straight and narrow. He told me stories about the Bible and what they meant. I tried but never really liked going to church or the prayer meetings we had to attend. I say that so you know, just because I didn't like going to church doesn't mean that I didn't learn and listen to their teachings. I looked to my father. He was very diverse in that he had several hobbies and was very good at all of them. He was an avid photographer and took a lot of home movies. He had a darkroom in the basement for years and developed his own photos. My father was a great outdoorsman who could shoot with the best of them. He would take all his boys hunting, and as soon as we were eleven or twelve, we got our first gun. Mine was a Stevens single-shot .22.

In those days, the man was the breadwinner, and the wife raised the children and took care of the home. My mom was the best at her job that I ever saw. She made it look effortless, and it really suited her. She was a good cook, baker, gardener, housekeeper, and a great mom. She taught me how to cook and do laundry, so when I went off to college, I knew these things and didn't need any help from anybody. I knew I was going to college in our town, so I would do laundry at home and eat a lot of my meals there too. But that didn't stop her from teaching life lessons.

There is another side of my mother that all mothers have. She was the "boss." When she asked you to do something, you had better do it or suffer the consequences. There were many times somebody messed up, and she would bring all five children into the living room and grill all of us about who had done what. If nobody fessed up, then everybody got the paddle. We were lined up at the couch, and she went right down the row swatting children. I laugh now because it would have been a sight seeing all those bare bottoms lined up at the couch.

Our town was like all the other little towns in Iowa. Everything you need was here. I don't even remember going downtown until I was five or six, and it was only six or seven blocks from our house. There were no big chain stores then, no interstate, so we all made do with what we had in town. The highway went right through the middle of town, and there was a Greyhound bus that came through twice a day, morning and afternoon. We had a train that came through also which brought passengers and goods to us.

I would lie awake in the evenings listening to the trucks come up the town hill shifting and grinding gears as it came. We would go down there and find ball bearings from the truck wheels and shoot them with our slingshots. The train came through sometimes at night too. Boy, you could hear it way down the tracks clicking and clacking on the old rails. I would try to stay awake as long as I could to hear it leave the station and would strain to hear it four or five miles down the tracks until I fell asleep.

Since we had the college here, we always had new people moving in and out. My father's business was good for that reason. He told me one time that he had sold the same house six or seven times in his career. I had to laugh about that. The people who came almost always had what my parents called culture shock because it was so small and had nothing to do in the evenings or the weekends. There are about as many students in the school as in the whole town, so when the fall came, the whole town would fill up, and there were people everywhere. I loved it.

One thing I forgot to mention was that this college was like a lot of small colleges in Iowa; it was a church college. I was the fifth generation in my family to go there. Since it is a private college, there are greater bonds between the alumni and the college because the college counts on the donations from the alumni to fund a lot of the buildings and the upkeep. Here, again, everyone knows everyone. This helps when you are graduating and need to find a job in a certain field or a certain state. Alumni will put you up in their homes, feed you, find you a job, and guide you through your day-to-day struggles until you are on your feet. When homecoming weekend comes, in October, the town is busy with people. Most but not all alumni would stay with friends who still live in town. We would get friends and family staying with us, and all of us boys would sleep in my big brother's room to make room for guests.

Since the college and the town worked together to bring new business in, sometimes there is a problem between them. The college needs to help support the staff and teachers, and the town needs the college to bring money in. Almost like a marriage. They get along, and then they fight, and then they make up and go on.

I told you that the main highway cut right through the town. It brought all kinds of business from the people passing through. We had two grocery stores, dry-good store, hardware, two lumberyards, jeweler, bank, insurance, two restaurants, three barbers, five-and-dime store, drugstore with a lunch counter, bus stop, jail, movie theater, post office, two gas stations, library, ice cream parlor, pizza parlor, and a car wash. Through the years, they grew and then shrank. It was as if it was a living, breathing thing.

In the summer, all the college students left, except the students going to summer school. This was the time for the townspeople to have for themselves. This was when we would plant gardens, mow the lawns, have church ice cream socials and fairs, and do all the canning for the next winter. There were no air conditioners, so all went outside to do everything. In the evenings, we would go for walks, visit neighbors, go fishing, go for a drive, or sit on the porches and talk to the family. A lot of the time we would go in when the bugs got bad and sleep on the living-room floor, where it was cooler than going upstairs.

When I was twelve, I started mowing lawns for money and broke into the big time delivering papers. My big brother got me the job because he had a route and knew the manager. The papers would come in on the afternoon bus, and we would go down to get them. I think there were five of us that had routes. But first we would go into the drugstore that served as the bus station as well and get something to drink at the soda counter.

I remember the first time my brother, who was older than me by two and a half years, brought me to the drugstore. He sat down and ordered a chocolate soda and ordered one for me too. I was in awe of all the things to look at in this store. First was the big counter with a row of neat stools in front of it. Behind the counter was a mirror that went the whole length of the counter with shelves in front of it, and under the mirror was a cabinet that stored the items for sale on top. Shelves were stocked with candy, gum, chips, cigarettes, combs, and all kinds of little items that someone could steal if they were outside the counter. Then, there was the magazine rack with all kinds of newspapers, books, magazines, and comics. Boy, were there a lot of comics. We would read them when the attendant was busy with a customer. Otherwise, he would shoo us away.

I ran my route seven days a week, rain, snow, or shine. Sunday was the worst day because you had to put the papers together. The drugstore was closed on Sunday, so we would put the papers together by the door where there was a small overhang from the weather. The door was actually on the corner of the building, and since there were two stories, it was cut into the first floor and held up with a big steel pole to the second story. What a great old building.

The best thing about my paper route was, I had my grandparents for a customer. I always could count on being able to stop and get a drink or get out of the weather for a minute. The only day I could not do that was Sunday because they were asleep when I came through. The rest of the route was pretty much dull.

These were my father's parents, who were kind and generous people to everyone, and I loved them both deeply. I would love one more one week and then the other the next week. Weird, I know. My grandfather Martin worked with my father, and so I would see him quite often. Martin was a very gentle soul and helped everybody he could through life. When someone needed help, they all knew they could come to him, and he would help. My whole life, I have never heard anybody say anything bad about my grandfather. There have been many, many times someone would come to me and say my grandfather was a saint. Then, they would tell me what he had done to make their lives better.

My grandmother Pauline was a mirror image of Martin. I wonder how they ever met and married. One thing I remember of her was, her house was always clean, and everything was in its place. When we came to her house, there were certain rules we had to remember. Things like "Don't get into Grandpa's study," "Keep out of the bedrooms," "No horseplay on the furniture," "No food in certain parts of the house," and things like that. But on the other hand, she was a great cook and an even better baker. I loved her food, and she would always start a special meal with shrimp cocktail. The first time I ate it was at her house, and I loved it. It made me feel more grown-up.

Grandmother seemed to do little things for me that she didn't do for the rest of the grandchildren. She was a perfectionist when it came to her baking. Her best pies were Boston cream pies. She would take two days to make the pies for a special dinner, and everyone knew when you came to her house, you were going to eat these pies for dessert. What nobody knew but me was that she had mistakes with her pies—that is, when she would ask me in when I was delivering her paper and I would get to eat the mistakes. She always gave me a bottle of Coke to wash it down with. We never had soft drinks in our house until I was older.

Grandmother also asked me to mow her lawn. I remember it was 1964 when, one day out of the blue, she sat me down at the kitchen table and gave me a Coke. We were talking about golf. She loved to play golf, and so did I. After my grandfather passed away, I regularly drove the golf cart for her, and she would pay me with a cold bottle of Coke at the end of nine holes. Anyway, that was the day she asked me if I thought I was old enough and big enough to mow her lawn. I really wanted to do it for her, but on the other hand, she had a big backyard with all kinds of fruit trees, garage, flower garden, regular garden, and a real nice picnic table that sat under the biggest elm tree I have ever seen. I thought about this and said I would do it for $1.50 if she would provide me with a Coke after each time I was done. A Coke cost $0.10 then.

One day, after I had finished the lawn, I was sitting in the front porch swing when I heard a knock at the back door of Grandmother's house. I jumped up and ran inside to see who would be knocking at her back door. My grandmother had already come back into the kitchen and was taking out a paper plate, which she used when we would eat out at the picnic table. She was starting to make a sandwich and didn't see me come in.

"Grandma, who was at the door?" I asked her.

She turned, a little startled. "It is an old friend of mine who needs something to eat? Would you mind getting a Coke out of the back fridge and take her this sandwich, please?"

I went to the back and got the Coke and then came back to get the sandwich. Grandma was done making the sandwich and had put an apple and an orange on the plate as well as some chips. I looked at her and said, "Why is she eating outside on the picnic table?"

Looking directly into my eyes, her answer was, "She likes to be outdoors because a house is too confining for her. Now, hurry along and don't drop this plate jumping down those steps and mind your manners." My grandmother was all about manners.

I took the plate from her and went out the door and down the steps, along the walk and turned the corner of the garage where the big elm tree stood blowing softly in the afternoon breeze. There sitting at the table was a woman with her back to me. I came around the end of the table and set the plate down in front of her and put the bottle of Coke in front of the plate. Then, I sat down across from the woman to see what she looked like.

She was a big woman, about six feet tall, but not fat. She had dark hair and the prettiest eyes when she looked up to see me. She had light-brown skin and wore a summer dress that was clean but looked a little faded from the sun and washing. I saw she had a pack sitting by her, and there was a furry little white dog sitting on the pack, and it looked like she was guarding it.

I spoke first. "My name is David. I am Pauline's grandson." Then something I wanted to take back as soon as I said it came out of my mouth. "You sure are pretty."

She looked at me over her sandwich and just smiled. "What is the name of your dog?"

"Mia," she replied. "And my name is Pearl."

"Grandmother says you are an old friend of hers, but I have never seen you. Where are you from?"

Pearl just kept eating and looked out through the little orchard. She looked happy and a little tired. She had big hands, and the rest of her looked like she was a worker. She had big shoulders, and her arms had muscles like a man. I wish I had muscles like that. Pearl fed some of the sandwich to Mia and then turned to me as she picked up the orange and peeled it. After she finished eating the orange, she spoke. "How old are you, David?"

"Twelve and a half, my birthday is in October," I replied. I had a lot of questions for this woman, and something told me she would tell me when she was ready and not before.

Pearl started to talk. She told me she was from New Orleans and was born and raised there. She was Creole-born to an African mother and a European father. She told me she had seen me before when I was very little. My grandmother had brought me out to meet Pearl right here at this very spot. Pearl was a migrant worker who would go where the crops needed to be harvested. She would stay several months and would make her way back to New Orleans to her family in the late fall. All the while she would stop and visit people she knew, and they would feed her and sometimes let her sleep in a barn or sometimes on the floor in the kitchen by the fire. She had been all over the US and Canada picking berries, apples, grapes, melons and even worked at canneries in the northwest.

I had so many questions about the world out there and how it was like. We took two weeks out of the year to go on vacations each summer. My father would pull out the old tent to see if there were holes, and we would hoist it up in a tree so it could air out. It always smelled musty. We would pack the station wagon up with everything, and everybody would pile in and go from one coast to the other in search of fun and relaxation. The problem was, there was no air in the car, and in the evenings, we would have to find a spot to pitch the tent then cook supper. After driving in the heat all day then setting up camp, we would complain, but I would not trade these vacations for anything.

There was something special about Pearl that I could not put my finger on. It might have been the way her eyes sparkled or the way her mouth would turn up when she talked. She had a thick accent that I could listen to all day long. One odd thing was, she told me about her daughter and that I needed to meet her someday. When I asked about her, she would go on and on, but she told me she had not been born yet. Okay, I thought to myself, she is not playing with a full deck.

Just before I had to leave, she gave me a chain with a yellow-gold liquid in a ball attached to the chain with a gold holder like an eagle's talon. I later found out that it was called an amulet, and if you looked at it for quite a while, it looked like a small sun was in the middle. She looked in my eyes and told me to never take it off, not even when I took a bath. It was neat, so I took it and put it on. Pearl also told me she would see me again. My grandmother called me in, so I said bye to my new friend and her little dog.

When I came in with the plate and threw it away, Grandmother was in the kitchen washing some dishes. She looked at me and saw the chain and got a look of satisfaction on her face. She took my face in her hands and kissed my cheek then hugged me real big. "I see you have a new friend and she gave you a real nice gift," she said. I felt the blood rush to my face and got a real big grin from ear to ear. I told my grandmother goodbye and skipped out the front door, and I got on my bike and rode toward home.

The year 1964 was also the first year I realized we were in a war. Even though I was not old enough for the draft, it changed me. There was an urgency all around me. Like everyone found another gear and they all were using it. I watched from the sidelines like a team player as people moved in and out of my life and the life of the town. We would go out to the college on Saturday afternoon and skate in the student center, and that is where I met several boys who were going to war and several who had just gotten out of the service. I would listen to them tell about the horrors they had seen and relay to the boys who were leaving what to expect when they go. It seemed so far away but close too because this was the first war that we saw firsthand on TV. Terrible things that people were doing to each other in black-and-white right in our own home via the TV.

I want you to know this because, even though I never served (because in the draft, my number was 314), it had a lasting effect on me and all my generation. It was that we did what we wanted because there were no boundaries anymore. I felt that everything was out of control and nobody seemed to have the answers. It was a good time and it was a bad time for the American people, especially for the youth because we didn't know if tomorrow would come, and if it did, what would it be like? So when I grew up, anything went—no laws, no guilt. If you could think it, you could do it.

But for now, I was in my own little world, and I had other things to think about—things like "How could I get the money for a new bike," "When was the next Superman comic coming to my town," "What is for supper," and "Will the little girl I like at school still like me on Monday?" Like I said, those were the days, and looking back, I wish I could relive them all, the good and the bad.

I didn't see Pearl until the following year, in the summer again. One day, I was doing my paper route and stopped to get a drink of water at the fountain in the park a few blocks from my grandmother's house. I looked up from the fountain, and there she was, sitting on a bench under a shade tree. She was reading a book, and her little dog, Mia, was sitting beside her by her pack. When Mia saw me, she barked and jumped down and ran to see me. I petted her, and we walked back to the bench to sit down. Mia jumped into my lap like we were long-lost buds.

Pearl turned to me. I could see a smile on her face, and she looked me up and down like she was sizing me up for something. When she did speak, it was like honey coming out of her mouth. "Mr. David Hunter, fancy meeting you here. How long has it been since that day under your grandmother's tree?"

"I don't know, I guess about a year," I said.

She reached over and tussled my hair and said, "You look older. I bet the girls are all over you this fall in school." I blushed and lost all my words. When I looked up into her face, I saw that she was prettier than ever, and that made me blush even more, thinking that I was so close that I could smell her perfume. Everything after that was as if I was in a daze. I heard her words and the words that came out of my mouth, but I really could not tell you what we talked about. I think a lot of the time we just sat and looked at the world 'round us. I felt so peaceful when I was around her. Nothing else mattered, and I didn't need to worry about anything but staying close to her.

All of a sudden, I was brought back to earth by her words. "David, have you been wearing your amulet that I gave you?"

"Yes," I answered.

Pearl looked me in my eyes like she was looking clear into my soul for a long, long time, and just when I thought she was going to say something, she turned and picked up Mia and started petting her. "You are going to be fourteen this fall, aren't you?"

"Yes," I said, wondering what she had been going to say that she didn't. "Football practice starts next month, and I am really looking forward to that." I loved football and any other sport that the school offered. I was good at all sports and felt in my own element when I played them. I didn't know then that my father had already talked to the college about getting me a free ride in sports. But that didn't matter because I would have played for anybody back then and maybe paid them to play me. I liked playing guard on offense but loved playing linebacker and end on defense. I really liked being right in the middle of every play and had the bumps and bruises to show it when the season was on.

We were a little town with a little school who had a little football team. As a matter of fact, all the sports were like that here. I didn't mind because I got to play most of the positions and always all the game. I didn't sit on the bench ever. I was starting to get muscle mass and would stand in front of the mirror forever, looking at the way my body was changing. And the hair! It was starting to grow all over my body, and that was okay with me. Most of my friends didn't get body hair until later. One day, I took my sister's mascara and put it on the hair that was growing on my lip, and my father took a picture of it. I loved that picture.

Anyway, Pearl and I talked for quite a while, and then I had to get back to my paper route. When we said goodbye, Pearl said she would see me next summer. I looked back as I got on my bike and saw Pearl and Mia sitting there looking like they had no cares in the world. I smiled and rode on.

School started the first of September, and it seemed like it flew by for me. The only thing that seemed to be on everybody's mind was the war and the number of boys that were leaving to go to war. That was the year that I started seeing "hippies" around town. Most of them came to school to try to beat the draft. If you were in school and kept your grades up, they didn't take you for the draft. You were deferred. But most of these hippies didn't make it through the first semester because there were parties every night. I know because my father had several apartments that he rented to these people and we were always getting calls in the middle of the night from the police.

This was good for me too. Why? Because when my father kicked the student out of the apartment, I was paid to clean them up and help repair and repaint them for the next renter. My grandfather owned them before my father. He sold them to my father, and I was bound and determined to own them myself someday. With the money I made from cleaning these apartments, I would buy roll after roll of pennies and lay them out on the living-room carpet. Then, I would go through each and every one of them to see if I could find a SVDB penny that back then was worth over a hundred dollars. I did that for a long time and never found a single one. But that is how I would spend my Saturday mornings and early afternoons before I went to deliver papers.

My older brother was always trying to find ways to get or make money so he could get a car. One way he made money was buying BB guns and cleaning them up and selling them to his friends. I wanted to hang with my brother, and he always let me, but there was usually a catch to this. My job was to make sure the BB guns were able to shoot hard and straight. That meant I would have to go out about thirty feet and let my brother shoot me in the back with the BB. If it left a welt, it was a good gun and worth more. The good thing was, my brother didn't have much money, so he bought a lot of junk guns that really didn't hurt at all. The problem was that once in a while, he would get a real nice one, and if I thought it was going to hurt, I would run up to my room and put several layers of shirts on or put a National Geographic under my shirt when "we" tested it. If it hit with a wallop, I would scream bloody murder and make my brother give me a dollar not to tell, but it never hurt.

All his friends liked me, and so nobody ever saw me as the little kid. I was big for my age, which helped. He took me everywhere and taught me all the things a seventeen-year-old knew. My brother was one of my best friends until he needed money or wanted me to do something sneaky. I could usually get out of these by asking his friends if my brother had to do it when he was younger. Most of the time, he didn't, so my brother would quit trying to get me to do it.

In those days, the boys were "cool" with their hot rods, duck tails, white T-shirts, blue jeans rolled up in a cuff, white shocks, and their penny loafers with the new penny stuck in them. You have never seen so much butch wax. We would put a big gob in our hands and work into our hair and then comb our hair straight back on both front and sides and ended in a little tail right in the middle of our heads in the back and down to the bottom. If you were real good at it, the tail would flip just like a duck's tail. There were drawbacks to this hairdo. One was, your comb was so greasy you had to take some toilet paper and take the excess off your comb before you put it back in your pocket. Another was, you usually had to use some water to finish with, and when it was cold, your hair would freeze solid before you got to school. The last and worst thing was, it left a mess on your pillow. But with all that said, the girls seemed to like it too.

There were only two other things you needed to be cool and have a real nice-looking girlfriend on your arm. One was a great car with style. The other was a black leather jacket like the "Fonze." We all looked like him even before the TV show got on the air. There were several older guys, "twelfth graders," who not only looked like the Fonze but also commanded more respect than he did on the show. They were the ones who liked to rumble and were always getting to fights.

My brother and one of his older friends were good mechanics, and all the cool guys respected them because they could fix their cars for them. So here was me hanging out with the bad boys in town, and nobody ever messed with me. I think they did tease me about girls and booze and smokes because I didn't know anything about these things and really didn't want to know. But in my class, all the boys looked up to me, and the girls all wanted to kiss me at parties and such.

In the spring, my junior high years were over and on to high school. I would be starting my freshman year this fall. This was the year that all things changed for me, the year I would start high school football, the year I would really get kissed, and this year, my life would change for ever.

My brother was a senior this year, 1968. He and all his friends, who were eighteen, would be in the draft in the spring. The war was getting bloodier and bloodier, and everything was put on TV for the people at home to watch. I remember someone saying that this was the first war fought over there and at home too. Because it was all televised to us, everybody had an opinion, and they were always ready to tell someone what that opinion was. Everybody took sides and would fight for what they believed in. There were riots all over the country, flags being burned, people getting hurt and hauled off to jail. And, yes, there were the "draft dodgers" who would cross into Mexico or Canada to keep from going to war. The US was split in two because of this war.

I want to say right now to you that this is a story, but 80 percent of it is true. The only thing that you need to do is figure what 80 percent is true and what is not. From here on, you be the judge, but when it is all said and done, I will give you some clues as where to find me, and I hope we might meet someday and discuss what you think is true and false.

In the spring, I was in my last year as a paperboy. I had outgrown it and wanted more money. The money was in the hayfields around the town, and there were hay crews that were run like gangs. If you got in one that was profitable, you could make a lot of money. But that comes a little later, because first I want to tell you what happened with me and Pearl.

I told you that there was a railroad that cut right through our town and cut through all the little towns in the south part of Iowa. They not only brought things we needed to survive but also hauled people back and forth from one end of the country to the other. I liked to walk the railroad tracks because sometimes you would find an old spike that was worked loose or something someone discarded off the train and sometimes you find things you could trade for other neat things. I once found a real good railroad spike and traded it to a friend of mine for a pocketknife then traded that for a BB gun, which I sold for ten dollars. I felt like I had made a killing, and I did. But I learned later on in life that if you don't keep putting that money into something else, you will spend it foolishly.

This Saturday morning, I was bored, so I went down to the train station and hung around, listening to the gossip and throwing rocks down the tracks. I started to wander down the tracks toward the old trestle. It was neat, and we played on it all the time when things got boring. I thought that maybe some of my friends might be down there, so that was where I was heading. There had been several drifters and vagrants coming through in the past, and they would stop and make a camp under the trestle until someone would run them off, so there were always things left behind to see and mess with.

When I got down to the trestle, I looked over the edge and spit over the rail to see if I could hit a big rock down there. I walked down the trestle a little ways and saw some old clothes and other things lying over to the end of the trestle. So I decided to go down and have a closer look at this stuff. When I got down there, it looked like the law had been there and just grabbed whoever was there and left their stuff. There was an old gunnysack with clothes and other things in it. Then I pulled out this bottle with some brown liquid that was almost full. I took the top off and smelled it and knew right off that it was whiskey. I decided that I could stash it and see if I could sell it to my brother or some of his friends. Just before I hid it, I decided to take a swig to see what it tasted like. It was horrible, but I got it down, and when it hit my stomach, it felt like it would burn a hole right through it.

Sitting on a rock, looking at the bottle, I thought that maybe I should try it one more time to make sure I had tasted it right. I grabbed the bottle and held my nose this time and took a real good swallow. It felt like I had fallen off the rock backward and then sat up again, but I had never moved from that spot. Boy, that was a great feeling, so I did it again and again. The next thing I knew, I was being carried to the shade and felt a warm hand on my forward. I looked up and smiled and passed out.

When I woke up, I had a real nasty headache and really didn't want to open my eyes. All of a sudden, I felt something lick my face, and I sat up with a start and hit my head on Pearl's forehead. She let out a yell, and Mia let out a little yelp. I put my hand to my forehead and said, "I am sorry, I didn't know anyone was there." Through the haze, I could see Pearl holding her head as Mia was licking my hand and running around between both of us, seeing who was hurt worse. Again I said, "I am so sorry. Pearl, are you hurt?" as I stood up.

Pearl took her hand from her face and looked at me for a long while before replying, "What are you doing here, and what have you been doing here?" Then looking around at the ground, she saw the bottle. "Where did you get this?" She picked the bottle up from the ground. I looked at my feet as I tried to come up with a good answer. Finally realizing there was no real good answer, I decided to keep my mouth shut and see what she was going to say next. I sat waiting for her wrath, but it didn't come. When I looked up, she was still looking at me, but this time, she was smiling and started to laugh and laugh and laugh. Because I didn't know what else to do, I started to laugh with her. Finally, we were both laughing nonstop.

My head hurt so bad I thought it was going to pop right off or, worse, explode. Pearl took her hand and wiped my hair from my face and held my chin in her hand so she could look right into her eyes. "David, I know you are not going to be a saint, but don't be a little devil either. I want you to know more about your role in the world and what God has planned for you. But right now is not the time nor the place for me to talk to you about them," she said. Then she turned and looked down the way as if she had seen something that caught her eye. I strained my eyes toward the direction she was looking but saw nothing but a little path that came out of some trees separating the railroad tracks from a row of houses at the edge of town.

I had walked these tracks many times with my big brother while we were going fishing at the town pond that provides water for us. This is also the way out to the fields and farms that lay just outside town, places that I knew like the back of my hand because I had hunted with my father and my brothers through all the fields and row crops around the town. My head still hurt, but I had a new feeling coming on me. One of peace and calm because I knew I was where I needed to be and who I needed to be with at that moment. Kind of like the look on a child's face when their mother is holding them close when they are putting them to bed. My world is this town and all the people and things that come and go in and around it.

Pearl was watching as I realized this wonderful thing about my life. She kissed me on my forehead and looked into my eyes and spoke, "David, you are going to have a wonderful life, but along the way, there are things that you will do and say to people that as soon as you say and do them, you will regret them. So, be aware of what you say and do, and try not to hurt anyone by actions or words. Know that I will always look out for you and will always be close to you. Now, I want you to promise me that you will never take that amulet off from around your neck no matter who or what tempts you to do it. Will you promise me?" I was confused and curious as to why she said that, but I promised her.

I had to go to the bathroom and told her so. She told me to go around the side of a big tree about five feet from us, and as I was walking past her, she grabbed my hand and pulled me violently behind her. I hit the ground and instantly stood back up as I saw an ugly man with a big nose, black hat, dirty long coat take a swing with a club or a big stick at my head. Just before it hit, I was looking at his hand that was the closest to me on the stick. What I remember was the big rings on every finger and that his index finger was quite long and had a nasty black nail at the end. I really didn't feel the stick hit my head, but in my ears, I heard a scream and that nasty sound as the stick hit home. I can't put into words the way it sounded, but I can tell you I will never forget it.

The next thing I knew is, when I woke up with such a headache, it made me vomit all over myself. I really couldn't open my eyes because any light would send me vomiting again. I would go in and out of consciousness. The next thing I really knew was, one day I woke up and my head didn't hurt anymore, but my whole body was aching. There was my mother, father, grandparents, and a doctor around my bed. My mother and grandmother were both crying and my father and grandfather were just smiling and looking at me. The doctor stepped up and shined a small flashlight into my eyes and felt all round my head. Nothing really hurt when he did that and I was glad.

He asked, "Does it hurt anywhere?"

I said, "It hurts all over everywhere except my head."

He smiled and looked at my parents then he said, "It was just from you being in that bed for the last several months."

My next thought was that I was terribly hungry so I told the doctor that I was hungry and that made everybody laugh.

The doctor asked, "What was the last thing I had remembered?" I said, "I don't remember much of anything."

They all looked at each other. The doctor said, "That was understandable when you have been hit on the head as hard as you were." It was as if I was leading a new and different life. I didn't remem-

ber anything about that day: not getting up eating breakfast, going to the train station, under the bridge, drinking nothing. After I had gotten something to eat, my parents and grandparents, both sets, got their chairs arranged around me and finally told me that I had been in a coma for two months. It was July. I looked out the window and saw that the grass and the sky and it all looked like any other day. Nobody but nobody told me about Pearl. They all talked about what had happened in my little town in those two months, who had died, who had moved away, who had moved in, and what movies were playing. I told my mother I was tired, and they all smiled and got up one by one and kissed me on my checks and patted my arm or chest and said they would see me tomorrow. My mother and father were the last to go, and my mother was having second thoughts about going. I told her I was okay and I was just going to sleep and would see her in the morning. So she left, and I drifted off to sleep.

I woke with a start and felt like something was chasing me. I was covered in sweat, and I couldn't get my bearings. I hopped out of bed and opened the door to a well-lit long hallway, and then I smelled the smell and realized I was in the hospital. I closed the door and went back to bed but didn't go right back to sleep. Something was bothering me, but I didn't know what it was. As I lay there, I tried and tried to remember what had happened to me that day, but nothing came, and then I drifted back into sleep.

The next morning, it was sunny outside, and I felt like getting up and walking the halls for a little exercise. My muscles stopped aching and started to relax the more I walked. Finally, the nurse stopped me and told me my breakfast was on my table in my room. I was hungry, so I made a beeline to my room and ate everything on my plate. It was weird because I couldn't get enough milk and asked for more, and they gave it to me. It tasted so good that even after I had drank four cartons, I was still wanting more. Finally, the nurse refused to go get me more until I saw the doctor. That was okay because I had the TV on and I got into the news about the war.

The doctor came in and asked me how I felt, and I told him I couldn't get enough milk. He looked puzzled but told the nurse it was okay for me to have as much as I wanted. Man, did I drink the milk in the next two days. It seemed I was always going to the bathroom because of that. The food tasted great too, and everybody told me it was not great food at the hospital. It tasted great to me. I guess it was because they had been feeding me through a tube or something.

My grandmother Pauline came in to see me after the doctor had left and gave me a great big hug and gave me a Coke from her purse. We laughed about that, and then she asked me a strange question. "David, did you remember anything about the day under the bridge?" I told her no. And then she asked, "Do you remember if there was anyone else with you under the bridge?" I said no again. She smiled and then on to something else, but I wanted to ask her a question.

"Grandmother, was someone else under the bridge with me?" She looked in my eyes for a long while then said, "Why would I know if there was or not?"

"Because I know you, Grandmother, and usually, when you ask me a question, you always know the answer before you ask."

She smiled a little knowing smile then said, "David, there are things we need to discuss, but now is not the right place or time. When you are out of the hospital, come and see me, and we will sit and talk." Now I was really puzzled.

Just then, my mother popped her head in and came and sat on the bed next to me. She hugged me and squeezed me until I thought I would lose my breakfast. We all talked about what a great day it was and that the doctor said he wanted me to stay one more day before going home. I was happy because I wanted to see my brothers and sisters and my friends. We made small talk, and my mom had brought a whole bag of comics for me that my friends and family had brought when I was first in the hospital. That was great, so as I looked over my new cache of comics, my grandmother and mother talked. Really, I was in my own little world with the comics and couldn't tell you what they talked about.

The next day, the doctor wanted to check my vital signs, weigh me, and check my height, so he took me and my mother into an exam room and take all the stats. When he got done, he smiled at me and my mother and said, "Well, David, I found out why you are drinking all that milk." We looked at the doctor for the answer. "You have grown four inches in the last several months. A growth spurt." Mom looked at me and laughed, and so did the doctor and I. Wow, four inches. I was really wanting to go then. I wanted to see if I was taller than my older brother now.

When I got home, everybody was there. I mean all my family. There were about forty people in the house all talking to me at once. I sat at the table in the dining room and had all my aunts, uncles, cousins, brothers, sisters, neighbors, and the milkman come around and grab, kiss, squeeze, fluff, and pinch me for the rest of the afternoon into the night. When it was all over, it was all I could do to climb the stairs to go to bed.

The next morning, I hurried and ate my breakfast then grabbed my bicycle and headed off to my grandmother's house. When I came through the door, she was in the kitchen clearing the morning breakfast dishes away from the table. I sat down with a thud on the first kitchen chair and waited for her to finish her dishes. She sure took her time. When everything was done and put away, she turned and came sat in the chair next to me. She knew what I was there for but didn't give any information to me until she got some from me first.

Grandmother started with, "David, there are people that come into our lives that help us through the bad times and celebrate the good times with us. Pearl is one of those people and much, much more. She is like a guardian angel for you and me. She watches out for us that no harm comes to us. That is why I know she was with you under the bridge when you were knocked out." I looked at Pauline and realized she was right. Pearl had been there, and for some reason, I had forgotten her and Mia. Why had I not remembered that? Pauline continued, "You will see Pearl and Mia again." Grandmother knew more than she was telling, but it was all I needed to know to keep from asking questions.

When I got home, my mother was sitting, talking to a man in a uniform, and when she saw me, she brought me into the living room and introduced me to him. He was the sheriff of the county, and he wanted to talk to me about what had happened under the bridge that morning. He knew that I had been drinking that morning and wanted to know where I had gotten the alcohol, so I told him that I had found it and tried it. Tried it until I passed out from it. He smiled toward my mother and then asked me who else was there under the bridge. I told him a friend named Pearl and her dog named Mia and the man who had hit me with the stick.

The sheriff wanted to know what the man looked like and if there were any odd things about him that I could remember. I told him that he was dirty and that his clothes were dirty. I also told him about the black hat, the long trench coat, and the hand that had one finger longer than the others with the black nail on it. When I said that, he asked me again to describe the man. I did, and he looked at my mother and said, "I don't think he will be bothering you anymore." I asked why, and he told me that same day his officers chased a man down the tracks about a mile from where I was beaten. The man fit the description I had given the sheriff. The sheriff continued to say that they were just about to catch him when he jumped into the river and they never found the body. The sheriff thanked me and told me not to be down under the bridge again and then added, "And if I catch you drinking, there will be hell to pay for you." I got his drift. When he got up to leave, he thanked my mother and bent down to shake my hand. When he did, a small chain popped out between two buttons on his shirt, and on the end was an amulet just like mine. He looked at me and winked and put it back into his shirt then left.

The doctor OK'd me to start working in the hayfields and also said I could start practice for football in late August with my team. I was so excited that I nearly forgot about Pearl and Mia. I was going to play varsity this year. I didn't care if I was on the bench or not as long as I was on the varsity. I had made it to the big leagues. The rest of the summer went by so fast, and I gained more strength every day I was in the hayfields. In the fall, I would be ready.

Since the school was so small, we only had thirty guys come out for football that year, and I loved every minute of it. All the seniors were good friends of my brother, so they never razed me like they did the other freshmen. They played dirty jokes on all my friends, and several of them quit because of it. I felt lucky both because they didn't mess with me, and best of all, I had made first string right guard right next to one of my brother's best friends. I also tried out for middle linebacker and got to play both offense and defense. I liked offense but loved defense. The coaches all told me I was a natural linebacker.

I didn't care if I made the tackle as long as I could slow them up so someone else on my team could take them down. Like I said earlier, the coaches at the college were talking to my dad around coffee at the coffee shop. My life was planned for me, I thought. First I would get through high school win a scholarship to college and then go into business with my father and grandfather. Well, that was the plan, but sometimes plans change. It was going along great until my sophomore year. I was practicing one day, and the coach was running a tackling drill for the whole team. It was my turn, and so I stepped up, and when the man ran at me with the ball, I reached out and tackled him, except when I did, I overextended my arm and dislocated my shoulder. It went right back into the socket, but the damage was done. They iced it, and I played several more games with ice and my arm taped to my chest so I would not do it again. The problem was, the last game I played, a man got through the line just off the center, and I was the only one there to stop him; otherwise, he would make the winning touchdown. I was out of position when he came through the line, and the only thing I could do was grab his jersey. I felt the tape rip away from my chest and then felt the pain of my shoulder leaving the socket, but I held on until the other guys came and tackled him.

I was in so much pain when the doctor came onto the field that he grabbed my arm and put his foot into my armpit and pulled. My arm went right back into place, but the damage was really done then. My parents had the head coach of the college, and his doctor look at me, and they said I would never play again. I pleaded to give me a brace that I had seen before with a leather strap around my chest with a chain to my arm that held my arm into place, but my parents would not take the risk. My career was over before it started.

They operated and stripped a muscle from my back and tied it into my bone with holes drilled. The scar was not like the ones they have now with a little neat hole. It started in my armpit and continued to the top of my shoulder. The pain was so bad that they were giving sixteen shots each and every day for the first month. After that, there were pills and pills and pills. I guess the situation and the pills made me depressed, and I would sit for hours just looking out the window or sleep. I slept all the time. I thought my life was over and there was nothing to look forward to.

When I got back to school, everybody was real nice and helped me as often as I would let them. My friends were all there still, but I felt like an outsider. No sports of any kind, the doctor said. What would I do? I couldn't bear to be around my teammates because they always talked about sports. I didn't go to the games anymore and couldn't even watch sports on the TV. I felt like a man without a home or life.

Little by little, I started to make new friends, ones who didn't play sports. Remember, it was the late sixties and there were a lot of potheads out there. The drugs were good and plentiful. We all told ourselves that the world was going to end anyway, so why fight it? More and more of my brother's friends were getting killed and maimed in the war, and there didn't seem to be a point. My brother went for his physical, but he had flat feet, so he was excluded. I felt relieved.

I graduated high school in the spring of 1971 and had no idea what I was going to major in at college. The economy was starting to slacken, and there was no room for me with my father's firm. So I did what all the guys did. I decided not to declare a major and start the year just doing electives. It's strange, but through all this time, I hardly ever thought of Pearl and Mia. I kept the amulet around my neck because it was a good conversation starter with girls at the parties I went to. And there were a lot of parties.

I told you that this was a church college, and most of the 1,500 students were members of the church. This was where Mommy and Daddy sent their young men and women to get a degree, find a mate, marry, and live happy lives within the church. But the first year of college, there were all these boys who were trying to stave off the draft by coming to school and all these girls that had followed all these boys that the college didn't have room for them. The college handbook stated plainly that you had to be a junior with good grades to live off campus or petition to live off campus, but nobody was denied because there were people the college turned away for the reason there was no room. This meant that there were teenagers with their parents' money that were living four or five in a house who could not even look out for themselves, let alone a house.

This mix made for a wild and crazy party town. The college, the police, the parents all tried to do their best to help reign in their children, but when you get a little of freedom, watch out. Parents were paying the college, police, landlords, and anybody else who got in the way of the American dream for their children. Money flowed, and drugs were right behind or neck and neck with it.

So please don't judge me until you read the ending of this book. I started to make more and more friends who had known of someone who had or could get drugs for all these people who were looking for them. Yes, I became a drug dealer, and for what it was worth, I was a good one. I always had a steady line to my front door. There was a lot of us. Some sold just to supply their own needs, some for their little bunch of friends, and others who went at it as a business. I was the latter. If it didn't make money, I was not into it. The problem is that when you deal in drugs, you are always high, always at a party, and always one step from being busted or broke.

I love fall because it seems that is when everything really happens around here. Through the summer, the little town is quiet and peaceful, but in the fall, the college starts, and all hell breaks loose. One day, there are no cars on the street, and the next day, there are parents bringing their children to college. All the houses and apartments are full, and the streets are busy. It all comes alive in the fall. You can't even get to the bar in the tavern to get a drink because there are all these packed in it. That is one thing the war did for the younger generation. They lowered the drinking age from twenty-one to eighteen, and then they upped it to nineteen the next year. So the bar was full every night. And I do mean one bar. The town fathers would only let one bar into the city limits, so that was the hot spot. That was where all the boys met all the girls and fell in love. Nothing like high school. That was where I met my girlfriend, Eveline, and we have been dating for a whole year. She goes back to Florida in the summers to work and make money for school and back to college in the fall.

One day, in my second year of school, I heard that the parents of one of the students had started a head shop in town, complete with bongs, pipes, papers, tie-dyed shirts, and holey pants for the hippies. I thought for sure that the town fathers would shut it down within a week, but they did not. I figured the cops were just sitting in front of the store, taking names of the people who went in, so I never went in until, one day, I broke my pipe and needed a new one. I waited until lunch so there were not many people on the street and walked several blocks from my car and went in the front door. The first thing I thought when I got inside was, they were burning too much incense. The place reeked of the sweet odor, and it almost made me sick. There was one big room packed with shirts, pants, coats, dresses, and the like. Then, as you headed toward the back, there was a door with beads hanging on it, and when you went through them, you entered a small room with a glass case the length of the room. This was where they put the good stuff, the things I needed for myself and my business.

As I was looking around the glass case, I realized that I was not alone in the room. Off in a corner was a small table with two chairs around it and a hanging light over the table. On one chair sat a young lady who, in this light, looked like an angel. She had the best tan I have ever seen on a person. Maybe that was because she had long blond hair that framed her face and fell over her arms and chest. Her hair was as straight as a string and ever fine. She was reading a book, and because of the table, I could not see the rest of her. I was there for at least five minutes waiting for her to get up and come around the case to help me, but she never stirred from that spot and never even looked up when she saw me waiting.

All at once, a young man about my age stepped through the beaded doorway and asked if he would help me. He was a very nice-looking man with long black wavy hair and a pair of glasses that looked out of place on his face. They were round on rim glasses that looked like two pop bottle bottoms hooked with a wire and set on his nose. They made his eyes look like they were very small. We talked for a minute, and I told him what I was looking for, and he showed me what he had in pipes. I picked one out and returned to the main room and paid for the pipe and left.

As I was walking back to the car, I could not keep my mind off the young woman I had just seen. I had all kinds of questions and didn't know who I could go and talk to about her name, where she was from, if she had a boyfriend, and if there might be a chance for me to meet her. The other thing was, I already had a girlfriend, and we were engaged to be married after we graduated college. If she found out that I was even thinking of another girl, I shuddered to think what she would do to me and also the other girl. So I tabled that thought and went back to my day-to-day life.

Like I said, this was becoming a big party town, and there were all kinds of parties to attend. It seemed that I was welcome to all of them, but there were still people I had not met yet. So as luck would have it, the school came through with never knowing it had helped me and several others make connections to people I did not know. I found out that day there was a concert held at the school to kick off the start of the year, and it was being held next Saturday. I had a whole week to prepare. I had met guys in a band that all came to school so they could get an education and still keep the band together. So I headed over to talk to the drummer of the band and see if they were playing next weekend.

Shaun answered the door after several tries to raise someone. He looked like he had been up all night. When he saw me, his eyes lit up, and he asked me in. You could see there had been a party and it had not been cleaned up yet. When I sat down, he asked me for some weed, and I gave him some. He was all settled in, and puffing away, I asked him if they were playing at the college next weekend, and he said yes. I asked him if he would help me meet some of the new people on campus, and he said they were having a barn party out in a hayfield with several kegs of beer after the dance and I was invited if I would supply weed for the band. It was a right off for me, so I accepted his invite and let myself out.

My girlfriend had just gotten back from the summer, and I went by and asked her if she would want to go with me to the dance and the kegger. She can drink me under the table with beer, and I knew she would be up for it. She said sure, and I told her I would pick her up Saturday evening, but for now, I had business to do. She was upset that I could not stay, but business comes first, and besides, I really didn't like hanging out in the dorms. Saturday night, I drove out to the college and picked up my girlfriend, and we headed over to the student center where the dance was. This was also the place we skated in the fall, so it was a big room with wooden floors and a stage at one end of the room. I slipped backstage and talked to the band for a while as they were getting set up and gave the boys their weed for the weekend. They looked cool, and I knew it was going to be a great weekend.

There is something about freshmen that you can pick them out of a crowd almost with your eyes closed. The boys hang in groups like they did in high school, and the girls, well, they are a new breed when they hit college. They all wear the newest fashions, wear tons of makeup to make themselves look older, smell like they threw a whole bottle of perfume every place there is skin. Some of the girls look like skanks, some are the next-door girls, some are prudes, and others have no morals. But you get them drunk, and they all act the same. Silly! I love to watch them at the keggers. Most have never drunk but want everyone to think they have, and they all puke before the night is over at least once.

So I love watching people, and there are a lot of people here tonight. I want my girlfriend around, because being a sophomore, she knows everyone. She introduces me to most of my new clients, and the ones she doesn't know, the band will know when we get to the kegger. Absolutely no alcohol on campus. They will even kick you off campus and send you home if you make a scene off campus. So most of the regulars bring blankets or tents to the keggers and stay the whole weekend.

There is a curfew on campus, and the doors are locked at a certain time. You must knock, and the house mother lets you in after curfew. The kids draw straws to see who will stay on campus and open the doors to the dorms after curfew. All the kids who are in the drawing are freshmen who are trying to impress the older kids. It is a sight watching one girl or boy go in and out of the dorm-room doors after curfew because if the house mother catches you, it is likely you will be expelled. There is another way you can get in too. Most of the dorms have ground-floor rooms, and you can get in through a window.

After the dance, we changed clothes at the dorm; nobody wears good clothes to these things except the first-time freshmen and women. It is a hoot. Tonight it had been sprinkling all evening, and the barn was on a dead-end dirt road, and it is about a mile from the gravel road. Everybody walks, or sometimes there is a tractor with a hay wagon that comes in and out all evening. Tonight we got there with the band and rode in on the wagon. Now remember, there are no cell phones in the seventies, so you can't call a friend or give out any information unless you go to a phone. None out in the woods.

When you have to walk all the way in the dark up and down big hills, about 90 percent of the kids fall down at least once on the walk, and a lot fall down several times. The kids who have never done this tend to drink as they are coming out to the kegger and think they will get in cheaper if they bring their own beer or wine. By the time they get to the barn, they have lost most of the booze and look like they were mud wrestling just before they came. What a funny sight. Most didn't even think to bring a flashlight.

We sat around the bonfire and watched as these people come into the light and laughed so hard we fell off our logs or rocks. They were covered in mud, slipping and sliding in their new tennis shoes, and half drunk with big grins on their faces. I have never had so much fun without paying for it. The great thing is, alcohol loosens their clothes. Boys will take off their shirts, and the girls strip down to their bras, and some will even end up in their panties. Great, great fun.

After watching this for about an hour, I spotted the girl I had seen in the head shop. She was with the boy with long curly hair and the pop bottle glasses. I could see her whole body now as she stood next to the fire. She had long silky hair to the lower part of her back and wore a halter top and short jean shorts with tennis shoes on. She looked to be about five foot five or six feet and had the longest legs for a girl that height. I wanted to get closer to have a better look, but my girlfriend was watching me like a hawk. So the only thing to do was go get a beer and go the long way around. I wanted my girlfriend with me, because the odds were, she knew him or her and would say something as we passed. It worked. As we came by them, my girlfriend stopped to talk to both of them. The boy's name was Cary, and the girl's name was Samantha, Sam for short. After my girlfriend introduced us, she saw one of her best friends and just walked off, leaving me standing with the two of them.

I said to Cary, "I met you the other day in the head shop but didn't get your name."

Cary said, "That is where I saw you. I knew I had seen you before."

I looked at Samantha and said, "I saw you there too." Samantha looked at me and said, "I never saw you there." "Well, you were reading a book in the corner, and we didn't talk." She had the bluest eyes I have ever seen, and they just pulled me in. I hope I was not that obvious to her or her boyfriend. "Is this your first year at school?" I asked.

Cary answered for both of them. "Yes, Samantha is a freshman, and I am a sophomore. I transferred in the fall."

My girlfriend came back, and she talked to them for a while as I listened. As I gathered more information, it seemed Cary met Samantha just after she arrived and they had been hanging out together for the last two weeks. Freshmen come a week or two early for freshman orientation to get the feel of the town and the campus and have some special classes about their majors, minors, and the electives they need to graduate. I never did any of that because I was a "townie."

In the course of the conversation, I asked them where they were from, and she said she was from Germany, had lived all over the world with her mother and father. The other thing that interested me was that my girlfriend told me later that she was only sixteen. Well, how does that work? College freshman at sixteen? She must be smart as a whip, I thought to myself. We made small talk, and then I headed off to get another beer and talk to the guys in the band.

It was a great party, and I met several new people that were potheads who were looking to score some weed. I had just brought several joints with me because I didn't want to get caught with a bunch of pot on me. So when someone asked if they could try my pot, I lit one up, and they all passed it around to see what it was like.

That is one thing about free pot: nobody ever said it was bad, and they didn't want to smoke any more. I got several new clients, and we made arrangements to meet Sunday evening after we were rested from the party.

The rain got worse, and since I had set up my tent earlier that day when it was sunny and dry, my girlfriend and I headed off to my tent. We asked Cary and Samantha if they had any place to stay, and they said no, so my girlfriend asked me if they could bunk with us. I said yes, and we all climbed into my tent and finished our beers and smoked another joint before we went to sleep.

The next morning, I got up early to find wood to start a fire, and when I came back, Samantha was up as well, but the others were sleeping in. I needed to find some small sticks that were not wet to start the fire, and I knew about a brush pile several hundred yards down the creek where there might something that was still dry. I asked Samantha. if she wanted to go with me, and she said yes. As we walked toward the brush, we talked about the party and the crazy freshmen who were there. Samantha seemed to be a down-to-earth kind of girl who was very easy to talk to.

I wanted to ask her about her background and what it was like growing in Europe, but I thought there would be time for that later. She did tell me how she had come to this tiny college in Iowa to go to school. She said that she was looking for a small college in central US and she had asked her school counselor to help her find one. They had looked at several in a book that the counselor had, and she had finally decided on this one. What really impressed her was that it was church college, and she said she didn't think she would get into much trouble in a church college. Little did she know that this was one of the most open church colleges in the state. It had not always been like that. Even in the midsixties, there was still no dancing anywhere around the town. If you wanted to dance, you had to go to another town to do it because it was forbidden in the church.

We got to the brush pile, and I found several dry leaves and small sticks to start the fire with, so we started back to the tent with them. I felt so at easy with Sam. She asked me to call her sometime and we could get high. Great, I was in her good graces. As we walked back, she told me that her mother was German and her father was American. They had met after the war and fell in love. He had stayed in Europe, and they got married there and raised a family. They traveled with her father to wherever he was working, so they had lived all over the world. She was young and picked up the different languages wherever they settled. Sam said she could speak and write six languages. I was very impressed with that. She also told me that she was turning seventeen next week and that we were invited to her birthday party next Saturday.

When we got back to the tent, I made a fire and opened the cooler to see what we had for breakfast. I had been a Boy Scout with my older brother, and he had showed me how to cook on an open fire. There was a pond by the barn that I had fished when I was younger, so I had brought a pole, and I headed off to get some fish for breakfast. Before I left, I asked Sam if she would help by tending the fire when I was gone. I caught several nice crappie.

And when I got back, I cleaned them and got out the frying pan and oil that I had brought along. There were some eggs and potatoes, so I cooked the potatoes first and set them aside then cooked the fish with egg and flour to make a crispy crust on them. Then I cooked the eggs and poured juice for everybody. The smell not only got my girlfriend and Cary up but also seemed to have people coming over to see what we were cooking. It was a good thing that I had caught several fish, because I figured I fed at least ten people.

After we got back to town, I took a long nap into the afternoon, and when I woke, I was thinking of Sam, and what a wonderful time I had with her. Just me and her walking and talking. It just seemed right to me. Now I needed to find a good way to get rid of my girlfriend and Cary, then we would have a chance to hook up. I spent most of the evening on that problem but had no solution. Well, there is tomorrow. Just before I dozed off to sleep, there was a call, and when I answered, it was Sam. Sam started by telling me what a great time she had at the party and then started beating around the bush about why she had called. She was with my girlfriend in the dorm, and they had a big favor to ask me. They wanted to know if I would let them have Sam's birthday party at my house because it was so big and there were no people for several miles to mess up the party. I said sure, and they both said they would do everything and would clean up after.

Since I was the only one with a car, who did you think ended up bringing everything from town to my farmhouse? That Friday before the big birthday party, I bet I made four or five trips to town for this and that. The girls did clean the house, and since Cary had to work at the head shop, that meant I had all day with the girls. I would find myself staring at Sam when my girlfriend was not looking, and if Sam saw me, she would just smile and go on with her business. How did she not know what I was thinking, and why didn't she say anything to me about it? Good for me because my girlfriend would have tried to beat the hell out of me, and Lord knows what she would have done to Sam.

Saturday came, and everything was ready for the party. I had picked up two kegs from the bar because I was the only one old enough to buy the beer. We had food and enough chicken to feed a small army. I would cook it on the grill, and the girls would be around to help me get out to the mad bunch of people Sam had invited. It is always the same about a party. You plan on thirty or so and get a hundred. This party was no different. The food went first, and that didn't bother me because that meant I was freed up to mingle and party with everyone else.

I had started sitting on my roof, drinking a beer when I first moved into the house several months ago. It was so peaceful on those hot summer nights, so when I was done cooking, I headed up to the roof to watch the party below. It was great because nobody knew where I had gone but I could see everybody and everything going on below me. I watched a freshmen girl fall headfirst into a ditch of water and three guys trying to help her out. What a great laugh I was having. There were several fights between girlfriend and boyfriend and some between boys. I was laughing so hard that after a while, I didn't realize that there were several people around me laughing with me. My girlfriend, Sam, Cary, several guys I had just met were on the roof with me. Within ten minutes, there were at least fifty people on my roof.

The problem was that they were all drunk and they had never been in a situation like this. It was an accident waiting to happen. So I did what any normal person should do in that situation and got my ass off the roof. It was really funny when I got down and went out on the lawn to sit down and watch all the drunks on my roof. They started coming down two and three at a time. I guess it was like sheep. They all followed down, and it was going well until someone found a quicker way to get down. They got to the front porch and were jumping off the eve to the ground, which was about eight feet. The last one to go was so drunk he caught his shirt on the eve and ended up falling on his right side. His friend took him to the hospital, and I saw him several days later with a cast on his arm. He had broken it but said he didn't remember anything until he woke up Sunday morning with a cast on. His friends filled him on the details. The whole school year seemed to be a series of parties, parties, parties. And when the time came to end the year, everybody knew everybody, and there were a lot of new couples heading off for the summer. My girlfriend was heading off to Florida, and Cary was heading out west to work the summer so he could have money to come back in the fall. One thing that happened in the last several days of school was that he and Sam had a fight and they had broken up. I felt for him, but I was looking forward to seeing what I could do to hook up with her in the fall. God must have been watching over me, because he was the only one that knew what I felt for Sam. The day before school let out, I saw Sam on campus, and she came up to me and asked me for a favor. I reminded her about what had happened the last time I did her a favor. Someone got their arm broke. She laughed and asked me if I could help her take her stuff downtown to her apartment. I am sure I looked shocked, because she just laughed and said she was going to spend the summer in town.

I ran to get my car and helped her load her things into it. I drove her to her new house and met her new roommates. I had met one of them before, but the other one I had never seen. She was there with her boyfriend, and I got to meet him too. They both were very, very straight. We unloaded Sam's stuff into her room and sat down for a while. I told them that I was going to move to town too because it was too far for me to drive every day back and forth.

Just then, another man came through the back door, and they introduced him as the landlord. He had been living upstairs and renting out the downstairs, but he was heading home for the summer. They told him I was looking for an apartment, and he showed me the upstairs.

Sam came with us; as we walked up the back stairs, he told me about the place and how he had bought it when he came to school. We walked in, and it entered into the kitchen. To the right off the kitchen was a small bathroom, and then straight ahead was the living room. Off the living room was a small bedroom, and that was that. He told me the price, and it was only going to be for the summer. I told him I would take it, and I could see the look in Sam's eyes when I did. It was as if it was fate to me.

We had a great time all summer. It started slow because I had a girlfriend, but by the end of June, I had dumped her, and she was gone, so I could concentrate on Sam. She was very shy at first of my advances toward her. We did a lot of things as a group: me, her, her roommate, and some other friends that lived down the block who moved in when we did. She got close to Ann down the block, and they did a lot of stuff together when Sam and I were apart. I liked that because Ann took a lot of her time and she didn't need to run around. There were always men trying to hook up with Sam, but she seemed to like what she had arranged for herself. Casual friends were all right, but nothing deep. She and I spent a lot of time together too.

I got a job working at night at the bar downtown, and she got a job working at a new nightclub four miles out of town. They catered to the cowboys and their girls. A lot of big-name singers came and went through that bar, people who were not big names then but would become stars later. All their pictures were on the walls. Sam seemed to like that atmosphere, and I would hang out there with my buddies. She never dated anybody, and everybody seemed to know we were an item, but we still lived apart and never went to bed with each other until later. I knew, though, that she had feelings for me, and me, her.

What had started as a game, sitting on the roof, continued at this house too. We could get on the porch roof from my apartment, and since I never locked my door, I would come home, and everyone would be sitting, drinking, and smoking on the roof. I knew that if I would act like I liked another girl, it would make or break our relationship, but after a month and nothing had happened between us, I was getting worried enough to try anything to get her to commit to me. I would flirt with the other girls in the house, but nothing but flirt. One day, I was home and sitting out on the roof and her roommate came home and got on her swimsuit top and came upstairs to sit on the roof with me. We were drinking and having a little too much fun when Sam came home and saw us on the roof together. I know she knew nothing had happened, but it was as if a light came on for her. She had suppressed her feelings for me long enough, and I guess that set her over the edge.

That night, I didn't have to work, and she didn't either, so she came upstairs with a bottle of wine, and we just sat out on the roof and drank it. I felt great being with her, and I told her. She looked at me and told me she felt the same way, but she had been holding back because she really didn't want to mess it up. We ended up going to sleep in my bed holding each other, nothing more.

Our love grew through the next several weeks, and it just seemed to me the right time to ask her to marry me. She had gone to see her parents for a week, and it was the longest week I had ever known. When Samantha came back, I was so sick in love that when I saw her, I grabbed her in my arms and carried her up to my apartment. We talked all that night about what we wanted to do with our lives and how we would do it. I could not contain myself and finally blurted out, "Will you marry me?" It took her less than two seconds to say yes.

We went to bed and, in the morning, started telling everyone that we were going to get married. Sam and I went down to Ann's house and told her and her husband that we were getting married. I really liked Ann's husband, and I was thinking of having him be my best man. His name was David, just like mine, and we seemed to have a lot in common. He was laid-back and kind of quiet unless he had something to say. David had been in the war and was a door gunner on a helicopter. They had a life span of about three months because everybody was shooting at them when they flew and when they landed to take out wounded or bring in fresh troops. I guess that was why he was so quiet and seemed to be older than the rest of us.

We all got closer as the summer started to end and all of us were dreading going back to school in the fall. September came, and the town filled up with students again, and we all headed back to school. I was having trouble with my grades and was about to flunk out of school, so Sam and I talked and decided that I should find a job and just work for the rest of year. We had decided to get married at Christmas, and I would find us a house, and we would get out of the apartment.

The problem with that plan was finding a place in the middle of the semester. There were really not any options for housing that time of year. You would get one in the fall and the spring, but not in the middle of the school year? My father had several apartment houses, but we didn't want to be in an apartment. But one day, he called and had a job for me working on a house he had just bought as a rental. I went over to see the house, and we talked about what he wanted done on the house, and I asked him if it was rented yet. He said no; he wanted to fix it up first. So I asked him if we could rent it and I would do the repairs as we stayed in the house. He agreed, and that was that.

I waited for Sam to get out of class, and we headed over to see the house. We were both happy with the house and what was going to be repaired or replaced in it. Looking back, I realized it was just an old house with four rooms, a bathroom, and an enclosed porch. Nothing special, but what was special was the two people that were going to live there. When you walked into the house, you were in the living room, then if you turned to the right, you would go into the dining room and left to the bedroom and left again into a hallway with the bathroom on the right and straight head into the kitchen then left again back to the living room.

The first fix was the bathroom. I had to rip out the floor and all the fixtures and start all over again. The floor was rotten. We had to shower at the college for a while and ran to my parents when we needed the bathroom. Or for me, I just went out back. Hahaha! After I got the bathroom done, I started on the kitchen and took out all the cabinets, counters, and floor. I put plastic on the hole in the floor so no animals could come in and rebuilt it first. While I was at it, I replumbed some of the plumbing and closed it all in so it would not freeze in the winter. Then, on to the cabinets and counters, put down the flooring and set all the appliances back in the kitchen, and we were done.

December came, and we got married on December 31. It was a snowy day, and we didn't think anybody would come. When my grandparents came, they had two old friends with them, Pearl and Mia. I hadn't seen them since that day under the trestle years ago. I was shocked and happy all at the same time. She came and grabbed me and hugged me for a long time. When I looked in her face, there were tears in her eyes. She smiled and said, "You look all grown-up." I couldn't say a thing because I was so happy to see her and Mia.

Finally, I grabbed her hand and led her out into the stairwell to talk. "Where have you been all these years?" I asked.

"Not far, just a little ways into Missouri. I have a family now and am running a home for mentally retarded adults," she said. I looked at her, and she was as lovely as ever. She had that same glow as the day I met her, but she was prettier, more pretty than ever. I grabbed her and hugged her again.

"How did you know that I was getting married?" I said.

"Your grandmother called me and told me, and I was not going to miss this for the world."

I knew that this was not the time or the place to ask about what happened to her all those years ago under the trestle, so I just put that in the back of my mind for later. We joined my grandparents, and then it was time for me to get ready, so I took my leave. On the way to the back of the church, I stopped and gave my mother a hug, and my father gave me a good handshake. My father was the one who was going to marry us, and I felt thankful for that.

I joined my best man, David Lee, and the other men I had picked for my seconds. As I stood on the platform, I realized there was a light coming from behind me in the audience, so I turned to look where it was coming from. I got goose pimples and the hair on the back of my neck stood straight up when I saw what was making the light. There were about one hundred people seated in the church, and at least 25 percent of these people had an aura about them. The aura was all around their heads and shoulders and stood about a foot taller above their heads. It was so pretty I thought I was to going cry. All the people that had this aura were smiling right at me. I realized they were the people that had an effect in molding my life into the person I was today.

There was my father, my grandmother, Pearl, the sheriff, my second-grade teacher, my doctor, one of the nurses at the hospital, two people I had never met, yet, and the list went on from there. I also realized they all were wearing amulets around their necks and they were glowing too. What did that mean, and how was I a part of this group? Too much for me to process, and then the next thing I knew, my knees were buckled underneath me, and I was on the floor. My grandmother was there first, and then I saw my father and mother around me. My grandmother was saying, "He is all right, just give him some room to breathe." I felt like such an idiot when I stood up and brushed myself off. Pauline took my hand and squeezed it and kissed my cheek before returning to her seat beside my grandfather. My friends all patted me on the back, and David Lee guided me to my spot in front of my father. The wedding song was being played, and my bride came into view, with her father guiding her down the aisle toward me. From there, it was a big, fast blur the rest of the night.

At the reception, Pearl came to me and grabbed my hand and looked into my eyes for quite a while before she spoke. "David, I know you have a lot of questions about what you saw here today, and I will tell you that they will all be answered in the next two years, so please be patient and let everything unfold all on its own time. I love you, and now I need to take Mia home. I will see you sooner than you think."

I picked Mia up to give her a kiss before they left and had to laugh. She was not a she but a he. All these years, I thought this dog was a female. I turned to Pearl to voice my findings, and she was just looking at me and laughing quietly. She took Mia from me and kissed his nose and then turned and kissed my cheek before she walked over to say goodbye to my grandparents. Then she was gone again.

I had so many questions that I couldn't sleep that night. Never mind it was my wedding night. We were going to Florida for our honeymoon, but we were not leaving until Monday, and this was Sunday morning. My wife wanted to eat breakfast with her parents, but I wanted to go see my grandmother and ask questions that were burning in my mind. Well, I went with my wife and ate breakfast and made an excuse to go see my grandmother and left them to their own means for a while.

When I walked into Pauline's house, she was sitting, reading the morning newspaper. My grandfather was out washing the car before church, so we were alone. She spoke first as I was sitting down in the chair. "Bet you have a lot of questions that you think you need answered right now," she said. I looked at her and waited for her to start talking again. "Well, I don't have the answers to your questions, so you are going to just have to wait like the rest of us did."

"The rest of us?" I asked.

"Yes, the rest of us." Then she put her paper down and grabbed my hand. "David, I hope you can wait patiently for your answers." That was the second time someone said, "Wait patiently." What did that mean besides "I am not going to tell you what you need to know"?

"So you are not going to tell me what this is all about, the amulet, the lights, the other people like you and me?"

"David, have a great honeymoon with your new wife, and don't worry or think about these things," she said. That was well and good for her to say because she knew these answers and was not going to tell me anything. Pauline grabbed me and hugged me and guided me to the door, opened it, and pushed me out into the sweet winter air and then closed the door behind me. I looked back, and she had the curtain back and was waving and smiling at me.

We had a great time in Florida, and I was not ready to come home, but we were out of money, and Sam needed to go back to school in two more weeks. When we were in Florida, we talked about the future and what we both wanted our life together to be like. She wanted to graduate and find a nice place to settle down and raise a family. I wanted to find something I was good at to make a great living for the both of us. I didn't care whether she worked or stayed home as long as we had enough to live and raise a family. So when we got back to town, we went about our daily lives just like before we got married. Nothing much changed except we were not going to the bars as much, and we did still go to parties if we were invited. I was good at fixing old houses up, so I started getting more jobs, but I still worked more for one person more than the others: my father. His apartments were older and needed more help than most. Two of them had been my grandfather's, and they were built in 1891 and 1894. So you know, they were a handful, especially in the winter.

The pipes would freeze, and then I would get them thawed then fix the leaks, and they would do it again.

About the end of March, my wife came to me with a new plan. She wanted to go school in northern Missouri in a university where she could have a better education. She and her friend Ann would go to summer school, and I would work in Des Moines to get enough money to move us down there in the fall. Sam thought they could find a cheap place to live there, and they would share the expenses, which would make it cheaper for both women. I could come down on the weekends to stay, and back to work on Monday. I loved my wife and knew that when she made her mind up, that was that. The other thing was, she had never lied to me about anything, and I knew she was thinking about us and our future.

In the spring after school was out, we packed her things and moved her and Ann to Missouri. Ann's husband was not at all happy about this arrangement, and I could see it and feel it as we drove the women to their new home. He told me later that they had been having problems with their marriage and this was a trial separation. I felt badly for him because he was so unhappy without her. We stayed the weekend and then came back to Iowa without the women.

On Monday morning, we went to Des Moines to look for jobs. I had some friends there, and one of them said she would get us a job at the bar that she worked in if we wanted. It was good work for me, and I knew I would fit in nicely, but David said he wanted something else because he was afraid he would start drinking, and that would be the end of him. David found a job two weeks later working at a plant close to where we were staying. I can't remember what he was doing, but he made better money than me and worked a lot of overtime. He didn't get to go with me to Missouri much, and I knew that made him more unhappy.

As the weeks flew by, I started saving more money for the fall, and I felt good about our future. This was the summer of 1975, and at the University in Missouri, I noticed there were more drugs than where we came from. When I came down on the weekends, I would meet people that Sam had met, and there were several couples there from my hometown, so we had a lot of things to do when I was there. It seemed that the locals didn't like the students and there were some places the students would not go. But my friends had met a lot of the people around town, so we were welcome wherever we went.

I noticed that Ann had a lot of guy friends and they were starting to hit on my wife. She was young but had a good upbringing, so I never worried about her. I thought that if she did stray, she would tell me, and then we would go from there. Every time I would come down, I would look in her eyes the first thing and see that she was still in love with her. I knew, and so did she, that we were "soul mates."

Finally, in the end of July, we decided to look for a house for the fall. I wanted to find something that we could buy that would help us make the monthly payments. That would have to be a house with an apartment in it or maybe something that had another house on the same grounds. We looked at everything in town and didn't come up with anything that was in our budget. Sam's parents were going to help us with a down payment, so we knew what we were looking for. After two weekends of nothing available in our price range, we decided to try the little towns around the university. We could rent something to a student that had a car. On the third weekend, we found it. It was in a little town of about 220 people about fifteen miles from the university. The town was on a river that had been one of the gateways to the western part of Missouri. There had been steamships up and down the river bringing people and supplies for years. Main Street led right up to the river, and they had every-thing there in the old days. There were old stores lining both sides of Main Street for five blocks. And on the side streets for these five blocks, there were at least seven old hotels that nobody lived in or maintained anymore. One resident told me that in its heyday, the town had 3,500 people in it. But it was an old quiet town with old houses and old buildings with nothing but memories.

The house was just two blocks from Main Street. It sat on a corner lot which was one-fourth of the block with an alley running right through the middle of the block. It was a two-story house that had been a fine house in its day. There was a nice front yard with great old elm trees lining the street down the block. They were white elms, not the real bigger red elms that had been taken by the Dutch elm disease in the sixties. Like most of the houses of this era, the house had been built onto at least once and maybe twice. You could see this from the front of the house.

In the front of the house was a porch that went most of the way across the front. It had a roof over it that was supported by four-porch post that were very ornate, and then one side was attached to the house at the end where the house protruded out. That was a little setting area in the living room. When we went in the front door, there was a dining area that had four doorways in it. One was the front door, the one to the right was the doorway into the kitchen, the one to the left was to the living room, and the one straight ahead was arched with double French doors the led to back of the house. There was a big room through these doors with a bathroom off to the right, and straight ahead was another door into the last room at the end of the house, which to me was a study. There was just one more door in the bigger room, and that went to an enclosed porch with a back door to the outside.

Back in the dining room, we went to the kitchen, which was very nice and big with two windows in it. One overlooked the front porch and the street beyond, and the other overlooked the big side yard. The kitchen was done in orange and green. Back into the dining room, we went to the living room with its sitting area that overlooked the street, and we could see two more doors at the right side. One straight ahead, and the other looked like a closet door, but in fact, it was a half bath with a toilet and sink. The other door led us into the bedroom, which was very open and airy. The first thing I saw, there was a hole that was cut into the wall that separated the bedroom and the big room in the back of the house. I guessed that was for airflow for heat in the winter.

There was no central air, and the only heater was a floor heater that was built into the floor with a grate on it, which was to heat the whole main floor, about two thousand square feet as I estimated it. I looked around the main floor and found no more heaters in the main house, but I did see that there was an old chimney in the dining room. I had brunt wood before and thought that would be a great place to put an old wood burner stove.

We went outside and up the back stairs to the apartment that was on the top floor. There was a good-sized living area with a small kitchen and a nice, neat bathroom off the living area, and in the back was a nice-sized bedroom. In the living room, there was a newer electric heater that would do nicely to heat this smaller apartment. I thought that this apartment would rent for as much as three-fourths of the monthly payment for the house.

Outside there were two outbuildings. One looked like a little house but was about twenty by twenty feet, and when we went into it, we could see that it was a washhouse with hookups for the washer and dryer. In it, there was a small electric heater, some cabinets, and a nice black-and-white tile floor. Outside I saw that there was a root cellar door on the south of this little building which, when opened, led into a nice, dry root cellar for holding canned goods, potatoes, dried fruits, and smoked meats. Since there was no basement under the house, it was also used as a storm cellar.

The last building was near the garden area, which was just by the alley. In this building was a small woodshop that hadn't been used for years. It also housed the toolshed for all the tools to garden and the yard work. I thought I could clean it up and use it to do repair to the house, yard work and show Sam how to garden next spring. Everything we had been looking for was here.

Except, like I said, it was an old house. The house needed boards replaced on the outside, new roof, new windows, or at least new screens, yard work on lawn and trees, and above everything, it needed a new hot water heater, and I figured a lot of the pipes needed to be replaced because they were galvanized and break easily in the winter.

I wanted to talk to the neighbors because they always have things to say about the house next door or the one on the corner because neighbors talk to neighbors and they also borrow things and ask for help on the things they don't know how to do themselves. And the truth of the matter is, there was no law at that time for full disclosure. So I waited and came back on Sunday just before

I left to go back to Iowa. People like to talk about other people, and if given the chance, they will tell you the truth. This is what I found out. The pipes are bad, there is no insulation in the house, the apartment had not been rented for at least two years, the owner was a woman who knew nothing about keeping a house up, the taxes had not been paid, and she was in a real hurry to sell the house and move out. One other thing that piqued my interested was that, until a couple of years ago, she had run a retirement home and several people had died there before the state shut her down.

That reminded me about when I was in my late teens, my parents had finally told us kids that the house that we had been living in for several years had been a funeral home for almost twenty years before the people who sold it to us had moved in. My parents decided not to tell us that when we bought the house, but it was the most blessed home I knew in my town. I loved that house, and years after my mother sold it after Father died, I would go by there every time I was in town. There were so many great memories made in that house that we all were sad to see it go, but my mother needed to be somewhere smaller and more manageable for her.

Armed with the truth about the house we were wanting to buy, I approached the seller myself, and we had a very long chat about the short-comings of the place. She agreed to replace the roof, which I was not looking forward to do on my own. The roof had too many angles and valleys, and the pitch was way too steep to stand on. She discounted the house several thousand dollars and agreed she would pay the outstanding taxes, fix the plumbing, and pay half of the broker's fee. We were pleased, and I felt that I could handle the rest of the repairs myself. My wife had no idea even how to paint a wall by herself when we started but was a quick learner.

We moved in just before the fall semester started and decided that I would work on the house first and then look for a job after the rest of the repairs were done. I bought an old woodburning stove from an antique dealer in town and put it in the dining room. It was the best place because the chimney was there; the front door was close, so we could bring in wood from the porch; and it was central in the house, so the heat could circulate through the whole house. I also traded for a heat exchanger that attached to the chimney pipe and blew hot air reclaimed from the pipe. When talking to a neighbor, I found out that there was a wood mill about two miles outside town and they sold stacks of discarded wood off the trees after cutting it in lumber.

Next, we tackled the wallpaper in the kitchen, and I took off all the old doors from the cabinets and replaced them with new ones. There was new carpet in the kitchen, indoor-outdoor, that we decided to keep for the time being. We painted all the ceilings in the rooms and hid the hot water heater behind a false wall in the bathroom, and we were done with the downstairs for now.

I replaced several boards on the stairs going up to the apartment, rebuilt the small bathroom in the apartment, and had the heater cleaned and serviced. Next, we painted the ceilings of the apartment and replaced the curtains throughout the apartment, and we were done with that.

I checked the laundry room out, and the only thing it needed was some insulation, so I rented a machine, bored some holes outside, and insulated it. Then I did the same thing to the house. It was harder, because after working on my father's old place, someone told me that the walls had fire barriers, which were nothing but two-by-fours placed between studs to slow down fire that was moving up the inside of the walls. I would drill a hole up top of the wall and drill another on at the bottom, put the nozzle in the top one, and see if the insulation came out the bottom hole. If it did not, I would drill another hole farther up and find the insulation and where it stopped. It was really time-consuming. You plug the holes with plastic plugs and then paint over them to match the wall.

The next step was to find a good renter for the apartment who could pay their rent on time and in full. The first person to apply was a young woman who had just started school and was a freshman. She had a loan for school and rent, so she was a perfect match for us. She was single with no boyfriend to run up the electric and water bill. She was quiet, didn't know anybody here, and best of all, could pay the rent on time.

In passing, I tell you that this house was haunted with the spirits of the past, but they were never mean to us. They would let us know they were there and sometimes would even help us if we got in a bind. Little things, like one day, I got a phone call when I was painting the back room, and I had to go to work for a few hours. I left in such a hurry I had not cleaned up the brush or put the lid on the paint. When I started back home, I realized what I had done and was resigned to coming home to that mess. Sam had been gone all day to the university, so when I got home, I changed my clothes and went to clean up my mess. The lid was on the paint can, and the brush was lying on a clean towel, neat and clean as the day it was bought. On the wall where I had been painting were handprints in paint of at least five different hands—hands that were small and looked too old. Somebody was telling me that they were watching over us. I kept the wall just the way it was and finished the rest of the walls with handprints of myself, Sam, and friends that would come to see us.

Another time, Sam had been baking cookies and had gone to the bathroom. When washing her hands, she saw some flour in her hair, so she stopped and washed it in the sink before she went back to the kitchen. She said she had been gone about twenty minutes and forgot to take out of the oven the cookies that she was baking. When she got back, there were the cookies on a cooling rack on the table. They were just perfect, except each one had a bite taken out of it and put back on the rack. There was a smiley face drawn in the flour on the table beside the cookies.

Sometimes in the middle of night, I would wake up and feel like there was someone on the head of the bed watching me. I felt safe, so I would just smile and go back to sleep. Sam said she would feel someone pulling her covers up and tucking them under her chin often. We never felt threatened or in danger in any way from these souls. They were just part of this house like the front porch or the toilet. We wouldn't have had it any other way. It was normal.

Now, I needed to find a job. Charles, the man who had told me about the wood mill, suggested that I apply at the university where he worked as a groundskeeper. I took his advice and applied the next day. A week later, I got a call for an interview with the manager of the grounds crew. When I went into the interview, I was very comfortable with the manager. He looked like he was about my age and was a very pleasant person to talk to. I gave him my résumé, and we talked about my skills, and then he asked me a weird question.

He asked, "What have you heard about me?"

I replied, in truth, "Nothing, I just moved here and don't know anybody but my wife and a few friends." I could see he was relieved, and he took a few minutes to think something over before he said, "Most people at the university don't like me much. They think I got this job because I know someone on the board, but that is not true. I worked for this job just like anybody else. I just don't want you to listen to the lies they spread about me." I assured him that I was just here to work, and I didn't listen to the gossip people spread about other people. I got the job. One problem about the job was, it only paid once a month. The good thing was, I and my wife would have insurance for the first time in our married lives, and she could go to school for nothing starting in the spring semester because I worked for the university now. I could hardly wait to tell her.

I found Sam at the student union after the interview and told the good news. She was very happy because she had some news too. She had been talking to her adviser, and they had decided that Sam needed to split her love of teaching and the five languages she spoke into two majors so she would have a better chance of getting a real good job after she graduated. This would mean more classes and more studying for her, but I knew she could do well. Sam loved learning and seemed to be real good at it. One time she told me her IQ was 160, and I could believe it, but sometimes people that have a higher-than-average IQ seem to be clumsy. She would walk right into doors, slip and fall for no reason, leave things or lose things all the time, forget where she was going from one room to another, and the big one was, forget she had a meeting or where she needed to be at one time or another. But I loved her, and I tried to keep her safe and on the right track.

She wanted to learn to bake cookies and cakes, so I decided I would teach her how to do that. One weekend, we laid out all the stuff to make some cookies, and I went through the steps with her in a cookbook. When it called for her to preheat the oven, she didn't know how to do that, so I showed her the steps. On our oven, there is no pilot light to start the burners, so you have to take a match and light it by hand, so I showed her how to do that. You actually have to open the gas to the oven and put a lit match into the hole to light it. It makes a little puffing noise when it is lit, and then you turn the gas up, and it heats the oven. No big deal. Sam followed the directions to a T, and we had plenty of cookies to eat and take to school.

Since Sam was going to have more classes, we decided she would take her car, the Beetle, to school, and I talked to Charles to see if I could give him money each week for gas and ride with him. He said he was happy to have company for the thirteen-to fifteen-mile trip to school and then back. Charles was an older man, about fifty, who had a wife and a beautiful daughter, about twenty-two years old. He was big, but not fat, tall and looked like he used to love fighting and drinking when he was younger. I say that because his nose was pushed over to one side like it had been broken and his two lower teeth in the front were gone. It made him lisp when he had to form certain words, and every once in a while, he would spit just a little when he talked. I grew to love that man and his words of wisdom. He became like a father to me.

Charles was on the mowing crew, and since I had laid concrete, they put me on the sidewalks and roads crew. We all picked up trash for the whole campus each morning, so he and I would head off to the west side and spend an hour or two in the early morning talking and picking up trash around the dorms and the parking lots. We would laugh when we would get to girls' dorms because we always find panties and used condoms that the students had thrown out the windows the night before. It was so funny because these same girls would see us picking up this stuff up and giggle to their girlfriends as they walked by, but the next day, there they would be on the ground again.

I guess I worked at the university for two years before Sam graduated in the spring of 1976 with her 4.0 GPA. I was so proud of her that I would burst. She was offered a job in the UN translating for some of the UN members. We talked about it, and I realized it would be a great step forward for the both of us to take the job. She accepted the job on the condition that she would not start until August 1. That would give us from the middle of May until then to sell our house and find something out there to live in. We would have to get rid of the dogs, but we decided to take the cat with us, sell the furniture, and when the time was right, sell the car and the truck. We decided that I would quit my job the first of July to help get everything done and be ready to go find an apartment after the holiday. It was going to be a great summer and a short one.

Sam and I felt that whoever bought this house was going to be picked by the souls that lived here, so we never gave it another thought if the people who looked at it didn't like it. We knew when we brought the right people in, then they would buy the house. Sometimes I wondered why this or that couple were not picked, but we just kept it listed with the broker. I was going to be close because I had just quit my job, and we had decided to have one last party before we moved. The Fourth of July fell on a Friday that year, so we sent out invitations to all the people whom we knew and whom we loved. People who had been with us in the beginning, ones we met along the way, and family who would always be with us. After all, it was likely that some of them we would never see again.

I wanted it to be a special day, so I went to the hardware store, like I had been doing for months, to pick out a new color for the back room. It had become a tradition to put out a new color the first of each month to see what hands would appear on the wall. I would take a spoon and dip into the color then put it on a piece of wax paper and put another one on the top. When someone or something wanted to make a handprint, they could lift the first piece of paper and put their hand in the paint and make a print on the wall. I had a wastebasket there to throw everything away after they were done. I wanted all our friends and family to make a handprint today just for this occasion. I picked a new color, forest green, and brought it home.

My grandfather had passed away in the spring, and Grandmother Pauline was not well to travel. My other grandparents never went much more than twenty-five miles from home, so they would not be with us. Sam's parents lived in Chicago, and we would see them when we came through next week when we would go to rent an apartment and look the city over. So some of my brothers and sisters would be coming along with David Lee and his wife, Ann. Some of our closest friends from college in Iowa and the university would be there. I figured about thirty or so.

I bought a keg that we will put on the porch. I was going to cook out on the front lawn under one of the old elm trees. We would set up a volleyball net on the side lawn with chairs in the front lawn in the shade and some under a tree overlooking the volleyball game. The house was opened up, so all doors and windows would be used for catching a breeze, even though it was going to be over one hundred degrees. Friends and family would all bring food, so we set up four sawhorses with two sheets of plywood to make a table sixteen feet long. Hopefully, there would be enough food to fill it.

When the day came, I guided people to the alley and the north side of the house to park so we would not have any windows broken by balls or flying objects of any sort. I wore the coolest clothes in my closet, which was a printed cotton button shirt with shorts, and my wife did the same thing. We were a match pair clear down to our white tennis shoes. I did have my ball hat on, which was always with me, and Sam had some crazy-looking sunglasses on, which I hoped she would take off as soon as the guests came. But she never did.

I looked at her gliding through our guests and felt so much love in my heart for her that I had to go and tell her and give her a big kiss right in front of our guests. How had I ever met the woman of my dreams in a small Iowa town on a small college campus when we were worlds apart just days before meeting? She looked radiant with her long golden hair hanging almost to her belt with those tanned long legs and dark-blue eyes. It almost brought a tear to my eye. God is great, and the world is right on this day. I have everything I ever wanted and needed at this minute.

I made sure that all our guests made a handprint in the back room, and we had a long discussion when they put their painted hands on the wall about which ones were women's hands and which were men's. Sometimes you could not tell because they were so old or so small. We looked at all of them, which were about fifty in all, and marveled at who made them all. I had a list placed on the wall by the light switch as to what color was used on which month. It seemed that there were more prints made on one month more than any other one, and that was February. I remembered reading that was the worst month for people taking their own lives.

Everything was going well with the party, and I was cooking up a storm under the tree in the front yard. Sam came by and told me she was baking her best cookies ever, and I told her that it was too hot to be baking. She didn't seem to listen and moved off through the crowd of friends. I was talking to my sister, who had come with her husband. She had been telling that me our parents had wanted to come but, at the last minute, Father had a call to preach in another small town on Sunday, so they couldn't make it.

My back was turned to the house when we were talking, and I didn't see what had happened next. I just heard a loud explosion, and I was thrown to the ground, or I hit the ground by impulse. The glass blew out of all the windows in the kitchen and dining room and hit people who were close to them. I jumped up after the blast and saw all these people on the ground moaning, hands on their ears, and the cuts on arms, legs, heads, and bodies. I was in shock and didn't know what to do but stand there. My sister was by my side and told me to go get towels, water, blankets, and anything to make a bandage with. We didn't have 911 back then, so one of the neighbors came over and told me they had called the police and the hospital.

When I made my way through the wounded toward the house, I saw Sam on the porch right in front of one of the kitchen windows. She was slumped by one of the porch posts, and I ran to help her first. When I lifted her head to check her face, I realized she had a broken neck, so I called my sister, who was a registered nurse, to come and check Sam over. She said the same thing that I already knew: she was dead. She grabbed my face in her hands and demanded that I go get the stuff to help save the ones who could be saved. I looked back and jumped up and ran to get the things she had asked me to get. It was all a blur from there.

Police, ambulances, fire trucks, neighbors all came to help. I went and got Sam's favorite quilt and wrapped her body in it and brought her into the bedroom and laid her down on the bed then got in bed next to her and held her. I couldn't think and didn't want to think. I just wanted to hold my wife and sleep. Sometime later, my sister came into the room and woke me up. The police had some questions, and the ambulance for Sam was there to take her to the hospital. My sister said, "It is procedure, so let Sam go with them."

When I got up out of bed, the police were sitting in the living room, waiting for me. My sister went out for a minute and came back with a glass with a double shot of whiskey and told me to drink it. I did. The police didn't say a word about that.

The detective was named Wallace Emerson who interviewed me. He was a big man, six foot four to six foot six, with white hair and a real nice, clean-shaven face. I remember his eyes more than anything. They were light blue, almost gray, and they seemed to dance back and forth as he asked questions about the day. His first question was very flat and to the point, "What do you think happened here?" I was sure what happened, so I said, "My wife was baking cookies, and she tried to light the stove, and it blew up. What I think happened is, she turned the gas on and forgot to light it then came back and lit a match, and it blew up, throwing her through the kitchen window onto the porch post." The detective looked at me and then went out of the room and talked to another one of the officers.

When he came back, he asked, "Why would you say that she did it that way?" I answered, "When I was in college, I had a stove just like this one. There was no pilot light, and I had to light by hand each time I used the stove. I knew this stove was the same way because the last owner told us. I showed my wife how to light the stove when we first moved in when she wanted to learn how to bake cookies. I know my wife, and she is very forgetful when she is doing too many things at once. Since the windows were blown out instead of in, I know what happened."

The detective looked at the other officer and asked him if he had written it all down, and the officer said yes. The detective looked at me and said, "I am sure that was what happened and that it was just the way you described it to me." He got up and looked at me and said, "I am sorry for your loss, and would you come down to the sheriff's office to sign the statement you just told me? You can come anytime, no hurry." I nodded yes, and he left.

My sister gave me one more shot of whiskey and then took me outside into the late afternoon air. All the people were gone except her and her husband. There were two carpenters cutting and nailing plywood to the house where the windows once were. Someone had swept the glass up in the house and the front porch. I looked back at the house and realized all my dreams and hopes had been killed today. The house looked so sad and lonely just like me. My sister and her husband put me in their car and drove me the sixty miles to my parents' house because I could stand being there myself.

They had called ahead with the news, and my parents met us at the driveway. My father had called the doctor at my sister's request, and he was waiting too to give me a shot so I could sleep through the night. They all hugged me, and my mother took me up to my old bedroom, and I went to bed. The next morning, I just lay in the bed, running all the events of the day before around in my head. I felt guilty that I didn't make my wife quit trying to bake, and then I felt guilty that I hadn't come in to light the oven for her. I knew she might have had a problem lighting it. All this as I lay in bed.

My mother came and got me up and took me down to breakfast. We ate with nobody talking. The doctor came again and gave me another shot, and I went back to bed and slept most of the day. About 4:00 p.m., I awoke and wondered downstairs where my parents were. I asked them to please take me back to my home on Monday so I could make arrangements for Sam to be shipped to Chicago to her parents' house. It hit me that I hadn't called them and told them what had happened. My mother told me she had called them and told them. I wanted to fly Sam home to them, and I wanted to go too.

On Monday, my parents took me back home, but first we stopped at the funeral home and made arrangements for Sam to be taken to the Kansas City International Airport, and we would meet them there. My parents insisted on going along with me to take Sam home. We would stay in a motel in town tonight and drive down to the airport in the morning and take the flight to Chicago.

Next, we drove to the sheriff 's office to sign the statement that I had given on Friday. When we got there, Wallace was in his office, and he asked us in. "I want you to know that we are closing the case on Samantha," he told me. "All the evidence and the eyewitness reports lead to the same conclusion. She was just trying to relight the pilot when it blew." Relight the pilot?

"Why do you say that she was relighting the pilot when it blew up?" I asked. Wallace had a strange look on his face.

"Because we found baked cookies in the kitchen and on the lawn. We know she had already baked some and thought the stove had gone out. That was when she relit it."

"But, she and I had gone over that time and time again, that when the stove would go out, she was not to relight it under any circumstance until she got me," I said. "Why would she have done that?" I looked at the sheriff and my parents, and I knew they would not have the answer.

The Sheriff stood up from his desk and came around to face me as I sat on my chair. He sat on the corner of the desk and asked, "Are you sure of what you are saying?" I looked him right in his eye and nodded yes. He got up and went back to his seat. "Well, either she forgot what you taught her, or she just had too much to drink and did it anyway."

I didn't buy that and told him so. Sam had been working in a bar for some time, and I knew when she was drunk and when she was just feeling good, and Friday, she was just feeling good. I know that she was on her way to getting drunk, but she was not there yet. It didn't really make sense to me. But I have seen several times where someone had done something stupid, and when questioned about it later, they said they had no idea as to why they had done what they had done. I just hoped that I could get past this without picking it apart the rest of my life.

I signed the my statement and was ready to leave when I felt a warm glow coming from my amulet. That usually means that there is someone else close to me that has one too. I looked around, and there was no one close but my parents, so I just went out of the sheriff 's office and to the car. When we were driving away, I felt it again and looked back, and there was a young woman coming down the steps of the office. It looked like she looked right at me and smiled and then turned away and walked the other way. What I saw was a young woman between seventeen and twenty, jet-black hair to her waist, tall, long legs and arms, dark skin, with a face like an angel's. That was the first time since this happened that I felt relief from the week's horror that had become my life.

I felt like I was dreaming and, at any minute, I would wake and Sam would be back with me and all would be right with the world again. I thought about how I had been feeling just before the explosion. There had been so much love in my heart for Sam just before this. I should have run to her and stayed by her side the whole day, then I could have prevented this tragedy. I was so tired and wanted to sleep now. When we got to the motel, I just lay down on the bed and fell asleep.

It was several hours later that I awoke and made my way to my parents' room. I needed to go back home to get some things for the trip to Chicago and wanted to drive myself to the house. My parents won this one, and they both came along. It was so strange driving the fifteen miles back to the house. It was as though this was the first time I had been on this road. I saw things that I had never knew were there. My senses were heightened, I guess.

When we got there, the house looked very old to me as if it was sagging in the middle from grief. I felt that way too. I walked into the house and tried not to look left or right as I got my stuff out of the closet and put it into a suitcase. I needed to get some things from the bathroom, so I walked there with my head hanging down, not looking. When I came through the French doors, I noticed the light was on in the back room, so I just walked toward it and was just going to turn it off. When I came into the room, I saw all the handprints that were all over the wall with different colors for different months and events. This was our life right here on the wall, and I just started to break down and cry. My mother took me by the shoulders and gave me a big hug, and my father was there too holding me. I finished crying, and we got my stuff and locked the door and left.

Death doesn't bother me because of the way I was raised. What does bother me is not seeing that person for the rest of your life. It gets under your skin and moves around in your body. I realized I had a hole in my heart where Sam's love dwelled within me. I still had a mental picture of her in my heart, and I could play parts of our life together over and over just like a movie. She would never get older, she would never be sick, she would never have children or grandchildren. Our life together would just stop at the point in time that she died, and I needed to find a way to go on without her.

It had been almost three months since I buried Sam, and it still felt like yesterday. Things were getting a little bit better. I had gone back to work two weeks after her death, was still living in the house, sleeping in the same bed, and eating the same food as before. The house became the old friend I knew before her death. There were creaks and groans from her and always new handprints on the wall. Not as often as before, but I would come in and see a new one every once in a while and would have to smile. At least I still had good spirits around me that would continue the tradition.

I actually thought that someday I would come into the back room and see Sam's handprint on the wall so I could know she was still with me in spirit and looking out for me. I never did.

My birthday was coming in a few days, and I would be twenty-five this year. There had been another death in our family just last week; my grandmother Pauline had passed away. I was hopeful that Pearl would be there at the funeral, but she was not. I loved fall, the changes of the season, the coolness in the air, the leaves turning all different colors, and looking forward to Thanksgiving. The days are getting shorter and still warm in the day and cooler in the evenings. I don't have any idea what I am going to do on my birthday this year. Sam always planned my birthday, and I would plan hers.

It was early on Saturday; it was still dark, and I was still asleep when something woke me by putting a cold hand on my mouth and shutting off my air. I jumped with a start, looking around for what or who had grabbed me like that, but in the light from the street, I saw nothing. I had been having a dream, not bad or good, just a dream about an old house in the country north of town. It was on a dirt road with an old bridge leading up to the house. The house was covered with trees so much you might miss the house if you were not looking. There were no cars in front, and it seemed that the roadside of the house was shaded, but the sun was out. I could see through the trees that there was a porch wrapped around the whole house, and the house was white with slate blue shingles and shutters. I know I had never seen the house, but it was very vivid to me just after waking up.

Another thing I realized, I had driven by another house I had never seen, in my dream too. This house was in a town and seemed to be on the south side of the town. It was really out of place like a picture in a book. It was three stories high, long, but not very wide, and out on the front was a porch that went the length of the house, but it was deep. It had pillars holding the porch roof up that attached to the house between the second and third stories. The porch itself was just a flat piece of concrete that went the whole way down the house also. And on the porch was white chairs with people sitting on them, and they were dressed in white. These people didn't look like they were normal to me. Then I realized in the dream they were all albinos: white skin, white hair, and light-blue eyes. I could see them just as plain as if I was sitting in their midst.

I was sweating so bad that I got up and took a shower. I was awake now, so I got dressed and ate breakfast as I thought about what the dream was about. Sometimes you know it was just what you ate before going to bed, but I hadn't ever had a dream that was so real to me like this one was. So what do you do? Well, I decided to go looking for the two houses, and if I didn't find them, then that was good. If I did find them, I don't know what I would do then.

As soon as it got light enough to see good, I got in the car and headed out toward the north looking for that dirt road. I went out quite a ways but didn't find the dirt road, so I came back the same way. Something made me turn farther away from town and go west. Finally, I had gone as far as I could west because the river stopped me from going any farther. So I turned north along the riverfront, and about half a mile, the gravel turned to dirt. Like I said, I had never been here in my life.

After driving a little more, I came across an old bridge that had a hump in the middle and old boards that creaked as I drove over it. I thought the car was going to fall through into the creek. Just after I got on the other side of the bridge, I saw an old mailbox on the right side of the road, but I still hadn't seen the house. When I pulled up to the mailbox, I could finally make out the house in a grove of pines and old cottonwoods. It was so dark in the trees that I just saw the shape of the house, not the whole thing.

I stopped the car, turned off the engine, and just sat there trying to figure if I would get out and look at the house or turn around and leave. Well, I was here now, so I got out and crossed the road to an old gate which had a path leading toward the house. The gate creaked when I opened it, and the sound made the hair on my neck stand out. As I walked toward the house, I saw it had a porch which looked to warp around the house just like in the dream. The lawn was nice and neat, and I could hear the river moving back behind the house. The house was painted white with a slate blue roof and shutters just like in the dream. I walked to the front door and rang the big old doorbell that was right in the middle of the door, the kind that sounds like an old bike's bell.

I still had the bell in my hand when the door opened, and there were two older ladies standing side by side in the doorway. They looked like to be twins. They smiled at me, and one of them said, "Look, Silvia, it is Harmony's husband come to visit us. Please come in." I stepped in and said, "Ladies, I don't want to bother you, but I don't know anybody named Harmony."

The second lady spoke next. "Maybell, David doesn't know our granddaughter, yet." So they were Maybell and Silvia. Maybell did most of the talking, so I thought she was probably the oldest, but I could not tell. They led me into the sitting room on the back side of the house, and I could see the great big lawn that ran down to the bluff, which I figured was the bank of the river also. The view was like a picture with the bottom ground laid out like a bedspread on the other side of the river. There was a patchwork of cornfields, bean fields, hayfields, and in the middle was a big field of sunflowers.

Maybell sat down at a big table and motioned me to a chair, and Silvia headed off through another door. Maybell looked me over with her eyes twinkling all the time. She had a great smile and was using it as she sized me up. "David, we thought you were not coming until this afternoon, so we were not quite ready for a guest when you rang the doorbell."

"How do you know my name, and who is Harmony?" I asked.

She just kept looking me over until Silvia came back with tea and cake on a platter. Silvia poured tea for us and gave me some cake on a napkin. I thanked her. We talked about the house and their lives together in the house, but every time I tried to ask any questions about my dream and the house or who Harmony was, they would change the subject and go on. Finally, I just drank the tea and ate my cake. One thing that got my attention was the way they were dressed, just like the Sears catalog of yesteryear.

One other thing that I noticed was, they both had an aura that I could see. And I had that nice, warm feeling I have when I am around other people who have the amulet. After my wedding, I saw auras on some people, but most I could not. They had the same aura. I mean, it was around both of them, and when they moved apart, it would split in two, and each had half until they were next to each other again. I figured it might be because they were twins, so I asked, "Are you lovely ladies twins?"

And they said, "Yes." After about an hour with the ladies, I told them I needed to get going, so they showed me to the door, and both stepped onto the porch with me. Silvia spoke, saying, "David, you need to go and see Harmony and her mother." I thought they might have lost their marbles, so I said I would just so they might think I understood what they were talking about.

After I got into the car and drove over the bridge, it hit me. Why didn't I ask them how they knew my name? It was as if there had been a veil placed over me when I entered the house, and anytime I asked a question, they would lift a wand and put me on another subject. I smiled as I drove the old road that ran along the riverbank back to town.

When I got into town, I started to drive back home, then it occurred to me that I needed to go to the south side of town to see if the other house was here in town. Main Street was empty as I drove to the other end of town toward the river. Looking around as I drove, I wondered what each old storefront housed in the old days. There were about thirty buildings that combined to make Main Street, and some of them you could still see it had been a bank or a dry-goods store. Others, there was no clue. Someone told me when we first moved into town that most of the buildings were owned by the same person. He used them to store old furniture and appliances in.

I figured I would start on the southwest side and make my way down to the southeast side. It was going to be less than ten minutes to cover the whole side of town; that was how small the town was. It was a great fall day, and the sun was heating up the air, so I rolled my window down on my VW and let the air hit my face as I drove the first street from one end to another, and then I turned down to the next street and did the same thing. I had gotten clear to the river and turned on the third street south of Main and was looking to the left side when, out of the side of my eye, I saw a ball roll in front of my car. I quickly turned my head to see where it had come from when a young woman ran out in front of me, and I had to hit the brakes so hard it stalled the car.

It was her, the girl at the sheriff's office that I had seen just after I felt that warm feeling on the lawn. She was standing right next to my window, smiling at me. She was about five foot ten, about 150 lbs., had a nice body, great long black hair, long legs, an angel face, with brown eyes, golden skin, and a killer smile with teeth so white they would blind you. I looked at my car and turned the key off. When I looked back, I just couldn't stop from staring at her chest because she was so tall when she stood up, that was all I could see. She had short white shorts and a sleeveless summer shirt buttoned, leaving the last two buttons undone so naturally I was looking at her chest.

"Do you want to take a picture of my boobs so you could take it home and look at them in private?" she said.

"No, sorry, you are so pretty," was all that came out of my mouth. What a dufus. "You startled me, and I was really not wanting to look at your chest. It was just the first thing I saw." That was not any better, but I couldn't think. Boy, had I been hit right between the eyes.

She hit me on the arm and said, "You must be that creep we have all been hearing about. The one who looks into young ladies' windows at night."

Then she laughed and hit be again on the same spot as before. Man, did that hurt. "Well, don't they have pretty girls where you come from?" She laughed.

"Pretty, yes, but not as pretty as you are." I smiled.

"Are you going to get out of the middle of the road, or should I call a wrecker?" she said. I moved the car to the side of the road, and that is when I saw it. The house in my dreams was just in front of my car staring at me through the front windshield. I jumped out of the car and walked toward the house. This pretty girl was walking with me and looking at me as if I was nuts.

"Do you want to come in, David?" she asked. I looked at her, and all I could do was nod.

"How come everybody knows me but I don't know any of you?" I asked.

She stopped and looked me right in the eyes and said, "I am Harmony. I bet you have already gone to see my grandmother Maybell and my aunt Silvia's house." Wow, what land was I living in, and how do I get back to Kansas with Toto? Harmony took my hand and led me onto the porch, where, you guessed it, there were several albino older men and women sitting in their chairs, looking up at me, and smiling. She opened the door and walked ahead of me into the kitchen. She put her hand on my chest to stop me here, and she went into another room, and I could hear her talking to someone else. Pretty soon she came back and held my hand while an older woman came through the doorway.

It was Pearl. My heart leaped out of my chest as I saw her come toward me and give me a big hug. I had tears in my eyes, and I couldn't speak because my heart was in my throat. She looked older, but she still had a gleam in her eye, and she was as pretty or prettier than I remember from my wedding. I just couldn't believe it, and I told her so.

Harmony had been holding my hand the whole time, and now I could feel it, and it felt like it had been meant to hold me. We all sat down at the table, with her still holding my hand. I had so many questions that needed to be answered, and I told Pearl I did.

Pearl leaned forward and took my other hand and then started talking. "I was the one who was given the job of looking out for you all these years. Just like your grandmother Pauline looked out for me. Most of the time, you didn't see me, but Mia and I have been there through all of your life to help and protect you from things that would want to harm you. I couldn't come to see your grandmother when she was ill, but I was there when she died. I couldn't intervene when your wife was killed, but I was there. And, now I am here for you today to help you on a new path of your life, and I will not fail you."

My first question was, "What does this amulet do for me to keep me safe?"

"Before you were given this amulet by me, it had been given to me by one of God's own angels to pass on to you. It is the source of all the power on earth and heaven. It is what life is made up of, pure energy, plain and simple. Your amulet has more energy in it than the first atom bomb. It has a force field of energy that will not let in evil. That keeps you safe," Pearl replied. "You were put here on earth to do this task for the heavens above, and it is my task to make you ready so you can carry yours out."

"What task are you talking about?"

Pearl looked at me and got up from the table and went into the other room. She came back to the table and showed me a book that was bound with leather with gold leaf all around the cover. It looked very old and valuable. She opened it to one page and then put her finger on a name about halfway down the page. She showed me the name, and when I saw it, the hair rose on the back of my neck, stood up just like before. The name was my name, and after it was just one word: courier.

I looked at it and said, "What is a courier?"

Pearl said, "That is a person who picks something up from one place and takes it to another place and leaves it."

"That sounds easy," I answered.

"It is, except couriers usually transport something that is valuable and are selected for the job because they can be trusted with the valuable item. The problem is, when something is very valuable, people want to steal it from the person selected to transport the item. You actually have two jobs when you are a courier, one is to transport, and the other is to guard the item from theft. That is the job you have been selected to do."

I looked to Pearl and at Harmony and said, "I think I can do that with no problems."

Pearl looked very sternly at me, saying, "There is something you don't understand about this kind of job. What we are talking about is not normal people who are going to try to steal these crystals. They are actually abnormal. Abnormal to the point that they are not of this world. They are demons that will be sent by the devil to steal these stones for him."

"What?" I shouted. "What are you talking about? What are the crystals, and what do they do?"

"Just what I said. You have been chosen by God himself to take crystals from one place to another and leave them. If he didn't think you could do it, you would not have been selected before you were even born. And to answer your question, they are crystals, more like diamonds, but not diamonds. It is complicated. All I know is, they have the power to be written on just like a book, and they have all the names of God's people in this area who are able to pass through the gates of the kingdom of heaven. God's souls. If the devil gets them, then he will take these souls to hell with him."

I thought about that for just a brief minute then said, "Are you crazy? Do you really think I believe this for a minute? God the devil, demons, and crystals?"

"Pearl, I like you, and I really like your daughter too, but I think you have the wrong person for this prank. I am not biting on this one." Then I got up and just walked out the door, got into my car, and drove off toward home.

When I got home, I was so upset all I could do is pace from one room to another and back. After I calmed down a bit, I went to the back room and just lay down on the floor and looked around at all the painted handprints. It seemed to put things into a different light for me. I believed in God, and I believed in the devil, but I didn't believe that God would select me for anything but maybe street sweeper in the kingdom of heaven. I finally closed my eyes and tried to hear God's voice. If I heard his voice telling me to do this thing, I would do it. Otherwise, it was all a prank. As I waited, I fell asleep and was sleeping rather soundly when I woke with a start.

What had I seen in my dream, or was it real? I looked up at the ceiling, and there it was. A big forest-green handprint of a hand I had seen before, one that I would know anywhere because it was the hand that had taken a big stick and hit me on the head trying to kill me all those years ago under the trestle. I jumped up fighting mad. That meant that the day we had the Fourth of July party, that thing was in my house, because after Samantha was killed, they had cleaned all this room up when they cleaned up the rest of the house. The paint had been washed down the drain. Did this thing kill my wife?

I jumped into my car and drove back to Pearl's house, knocked on the door, and Harmony answered. I brushed by her and found Pearl sitting in her living room, reading. "Tell me about the demon that was under the trestle that day he tried to kill me," I said. Pearl looked at me and said, "So, now you believe in angels and demons? What happened to change your mind?"

"Pearl, I think you know what happened to change my mind if you were doing the job you said you were doing and looking out for me. I saw the handprint the demon left on the ceiling of my house the day Samantha was killed. He was there that day, wasn't he?"

Pearl put her paper down and asked me to sit down. I was so mad I sat but jumped right up and paced the room waiting for her answer. She finally said, "Yes, the same demon was at your house that day. His name is Bellamy. He is one of the devil's right-hand demons, and he is a nasty piece of work."

I plopped into the chair and tried to get my head around what is going on. I was furious, but I was still more scared than angry. "What do you want me to do?" I was resigned to do it. Maybe I could get close enough to this demon

Bellamy to end his nasty existence. What was I saying, and what was I doing? I didn't know anything about fighting evil. I would be shredded into little pieces before I could get my little yellow VW headed in the right direction.

Harmony came and sat on the arm of the chair I was sitting in and put her arm around my shoulder, which seemed to soothe me some. She was such a pretty person inside and out.

Just then, a man came into the room that I had never seen before, but he still looked familiar. Harmony jumped up and ran to him and gave him a big hug. So I guess she knew him. Pearl smiled when he entered and looked at me and introduced him to me, "David, this is Mia, my husband. I am sure you remember him." My jaw hit the floor, and everyone was laughing but me.

"Mia, little Mia is a man?"

The man was about six foot four or taller, had dark curly hair, was well-built and well-dressed, and had an accent I had never heard before. His skin color was the same as Pearl's, so I knew Harmony, with her pretty skin color, came from the love of these two.

"Okay, I believe," I said.

Pearl went on, "Mia is a fallen angel that has been here on earth for several years recuperating before he goes back into battle with evil. All the men and women you see here are fallen angels that are trying to regain their strength before going back."

"You mean the albinos outside on the porch are actually angels?" I asked.

"Yes, they have just gotten here in the last several years," Pearl said. "It takes them about two hundred years to recoup their strength, and it seems to take less time here on earth.

"What more do I need to know? It seems there are things all around me that I thought were one way and now I find are another. But the Bible talks about human beings lying with angels, and their offspring were over 425 feet tall, and I thought God forbid angels lying with humans?"

"It is a case-by-case situation, and when they are wounded, they don't have all their strength and power, then an angel can make a normal child like Harmony. Besides, we are married," Pearl looked at me and said. That had to be the reason Harmony looked like an angel to me and had such an unusual aura. It was white like a cloud but had light blue all around it. Hers looked like the sky. I sat down to sort all this out in my head, and Harmony came and stood behind me, stroking my hair as I did. It felt so good to have a woman's touch again. I got up and wandered outside to the front porch and sat down with the fallen angels. Harmony came outside and talked to them in a language I had never heard before, and they smiled and looked at me.

I asked her what she had said to them, and she said, "I told them you were the one that was chosen to go get the crystals and bring them back home." She smiled at me and sat there watching the day turn into evening. I didn't want to go home, partly because I was afraid Bellamy would come when I was asleep, but mostly because I felt so safe and secure here with these people. I am sure Harmony sensed this because she asked me if I wanted her to come too. I told her no; I had to sort through the day's events and try to make sense of it all. I got up and gave her a big hug, and she kissed me on the cheek, then I went home.

The house was dark, and I turned all the lights on and went to bed. As I lay there thinking about the whole day, my thoughts wandered to the picture of Sam I keep close in my heart. She was as pretty as the last time I looked at her on the porch just before she went into the kitchen to bake her cookies. There is one thing that I learned through all this, and that is, nothing is constant except change. People, things, jobs, homes, scenery, and your life are constantly changing. You either go with it or are left behind in a rut. I didn't want to be the one in the rut. I drifted off to a deep sleep.

Something woke me about 8:00 a.m. There it was again, a knock at the door. Wonder who that would be this early on Sunday morning. I looked out the window when I got to the front door, and it was Harmony. I opened it and showed her in to the dining room. She turned, smiling at me, saying, "It has been a long time since I have been in this house." I gave her a puzzled look, and she continued, "My grandma Maybell was here for a time when I was a baby. She lived in the back room just through these French doors." Can I see? I motioned her toward the French doors, and she skipped to the back room and opened the door. When she was in, it was her turn to looked puzzled.

"What are the handprints for?" she asked, looking around. "We started them when my wife was alive. A different color for

each month or get-together we had in the house. When we would get together, we let our friends put their handprints on the wall with that month's paint color. Then we started to see ones appear overnight. We knew they were the departed who lived here before, and it made us feel more at home knowing these spirits loved that we lived here and took care of their home."

Harmony looked around, saying, "There is something wrong with this room, but I don't know what it is. I was just a little girl then. I will remember and tell you when I do."

I closed the door, and we went into the kitchen so I could make coffee for the both of us. Harmony sat down at the little table I had made after Sam's death. It seemed to ease the pain when I worked in the shop making things for the house. When I turned away from the stove to sit down, I was looking at Harmony, and it struck me how pretty she really was, so much so that I voiced it to her without thinking. "You are so pretty. I see your mother in you and also your father. How old are you, if I may ask?"

Harmony smiled and said, "I am nineteen but am going to have a birthday next week, so I am twenty."

"I am having a birthday next week too. What day is yours?" I asked.

"The ninth."

"Mine is on the eighth." I laughed. "So, how old are you?" she asked. Smiling, I said, "I will be twenty-five."

"Well, my father is thousands of years older than my mom too," she said.

We laughed, and then I made toast to go along with our coffee. Finally, I asked her why she was here. She said that her mother wanted me to come over and spend some more time with them at their house. I didn't have anything else planned for the day, so I told Harmony I would be happy to come. Hopefully, Pearl is a good cook, and I could get a good home-cooked meal.

After breakfast, we hopped into the VW, and I drove Harmony over to her house. As we got out of the car, we were talking, and I asked, "How come you don't have a boyfriend hanging around here all the time?"

She was serious when she said, "I was waiting for you. Mother told me you would come someday." I felt my face flush but said nothing as I walked beside her to the house.

Pearl greeted me and showed us into the living room. It was spacious and very clean. There were several old comfortable-looking chairs over by the corner by a grand fireplace, and we all sat down there to talk. Mia came in and joined us as we chatted.

"Pearl, I was thinking about that day under the bridge yesterday after I left," I said to her. "And I was wondering why the amulet didn't protect me from Bellamy then."

"Because, as you remember that day, you were drinking. As a matter of fact, you were drunk as a skunk. When you're doing anything that alters your soul, you are weak to attack by demons and dark princes." She continued, "When you are young, your power is young, and when you start to mature, your power matures with you. The older you get, the more it protects and keeps you out of harm's way. Just like a mother hen protects her chicks, people like me protect people like you until they are able to protect themselves." That made sense to me.

"So, you have been protecting me until now?" I said. "Yes," she replied.

"Now I will tell you the plan for your adventure to get the crystals," she said. "You will need Harmony to go with you to get the crystals. She knows what to look for to keep you both safe from these evil princes and demons. And believe me when I say, they are going to try to take the stones from you any way they can. Their only job in this world is to wreak havoc and grief on this world, and if they get the stones, God help us."

I was quiet when she was talking. Now it was my turn. "I really think if this is as dangerous as you say, this is no place for Harmony," I told her. "And what is the difference between these princes and demons anyway?" I asked.

Pearl started by saying, "The devil is the boss of the underworld. He has a dark prince for each region of the world, and demons are under the prince to do as they bid them to do. The prince watches everything in his region and knows everything that goes on there. It is his job to bring souls to the devil and make sure that the angels don't get these souls. He will take souls from the angels as fast as he can find them. There are stones for souls called the Book of Names that are hidden in the world in each region. These stones are constantly updated to hold the names of the souls that are held by God, and there are other Books of Names for the devil.

"Since the devil took one-third of all the angels from the heavens and was thrown down to earth, he has tried to find these stones and take the names in them for himself. God has hidden these stones with the people and has angels whose job is to protect these chosen people who hold these stones. If your name is in these crystals when the Rapture comes, you will be taken to heaven without death. This is why, among other reasons, these crystals are guarded around the clock. Nobody knows where these they are placed, but God, the angels who protect them, and the people whose job it is to keep them."

I had a question, so I asked, "Is this the Rapture the Bible talks about when Enoch and Elijah were taken from the earth without death?"

"Yes," replied Pearl, "but that was not the only time people have been Raptured. There are hundreds of Raptures that go unnoticed because people don't realize it has happened."

"What do you mean?" I asked.

"When there is a suspicious death that is not explained, most of the time, it is a Rapture. We call them 'Spontaneous Combustion,' where the officials find the remains of a person who has been burned up, and there is nothing left or just parts of them left. Most of the time, it is just some fatty tissue and maybe some bones and clothes left. You will know because everything around this person is still intake. The chair they were sitting in, the floor they were standing on, the bed they were lying on are all still there unburned," said Pearl.

She continued, "When these souls are called up to heaven, there is such a violent reaction between the soul and the body it causes such friction as the soul leaves the body that it ignites the fat and burns the body up. Most of the time, the soul leaves the body unwilling through the top of the head. There are many of these every year. People are waiting for the Rapture to begin, and the Rapture has already begun. Before God comes back to earth, one will be taken and another one will not. I am telling you this because what you have been chosen to do is go and retrieve one set of these crystals and bring them back here. You will probably see a Rapture, and I wanted you to be understanding about it."

I had to think about this for a while before I was willing to commit myself to this plan. I would be putting myself in harm's way, and that didn't sit good with me. I have seen a person killed, and it was not a pretty sight. I am sure Pearl saw that I was going over in my mind what this meant to me, and she and Harmony were silent as I pondered what she had said.

Finally, Pearl spoke again, "David, I understand what you are going through because I had to go through it too. There are two things you might not have thought about. One is that somebody has to do this, and the other is, I am not sending you out alone to retrieve these crystals. Harmony is going with you to help." I knew she saw the look on my face when she said Harmony is coming too.

She said, "Harmony was chosen to retrieve the crystals just like you were. She has known since she was a little girl, and I have taught her all I know about the evil that lurks all around us. She has seen it firsthand and will be a great asset to you on your journey."

It was getting late, and I had to go to work the next day, so we decided that I should sleep on it and come back for supper tomorrow night. I left, but not before Harmony went out on the porch and talked about what was to happen. I realized when we were talking that there was nobody I wanted more than her to have my back as we go to retrieve the stones. She is smart, funny, pretty, lives around all these spirits, and has been trained by the best person to do the job. Not to mention we would be on our own to decide what our feelings for each other are and where we go from here.

The next morning, I met Charles at his house for the ride to work. I value his opinion, so I asked him in a roundabout way, "Charles, if someone asked you to do something that is dangerous but you knew it would benefit mankind, would you do it?"

He didn't stop to think. "I would say yes. If it will benefit mankind, I would do it in a heartbeat."

I smiled and said, "Me too." We rode to work in silence, and he never said a word or asked me what I was talking about. What a wise soul he was.

That evening, when I came to Pearl's house for supper, I was met by Harmony at the road. She was waiting for me and was so pretty that I had to kiss her on the mouth and hold her tight. She did the same to me, and it was a while before I let her go. She looked up at me with nothing but love in her eyes and grabbed my hand as we walked to the front door. We never spoke until we were inside the house and were sitting down to one of the best suppers ever: fried chicken.

I looked over at Pearl as we ate and said only three words: "I am in." The tension was instantly lifted from the room, and we had a grand time. We ate, laughed, and planned the trip to Chicago where the crystals were being held. We looked at a map and decided to go the interstate all the way. It would be about nine and a half hours at least to Chicago, so we planned to leave early Friday morning. I would have to make up a reason to be gone from work Friday, but I decided to tell the truth and say only that I had to go to Chicago to bring back some things. My boss knew my late wife was buried there, and her parents lived there, so it was settled. I would talk to my boss and get the okay from him the next day.

After supper, we all went into the living room and sat down around the fireplace. It was not that cold out yet, but the fire was very comforting to me that evening. As we sat, Pearl gave us some advice about what we were going to see, hear, and do as we retrieved the crystals from the person keeping them in Chicago.

"When you get to the place the crystals are being kept, be sure to do everything the person that has them tells you to do even if you don't understand the reason for the request. It might well save your life or both of your lives. Next, after you have the crystals, trust no one. You will only be able to look to yourselves for the help you might need."

Pearl continued, "Make sure you are never alone with the crystals, and if you are, hurry to get back together because there is strength in numbers. If, for any reason, you get separated, find a church close by and wait for the other person to come to you. No harm will come to you if you are on holy ground. But, as soon as you step foot out of the holy place, you are fair game to all evil. If you are stuck somewhere and can't get away, you must hide the crystals or destroy them completely before evil gets them."

"When any angel, good or bad, comes to earth for any length of time, they must take on a human form with all the good and bad of that body. They have to eat, sleep, relieve themselves, and breathe just like any other human being. This will make them like you and me, but there are only two ways to kill them, or they will be back. One way is to put holy water on them, and the other way is the amulet you have around your necks. You must touch them with the amulet, and they will be gone for good."

I could see Harmony was taking everything in just as I was. After Pearl was done, she got up and started toward the door-

way with Mia and then turned toward us and said, "One more thing, if you get to a point you have no other way to get home, call me if you can, and I will try to help you." With these words, she turned and left the room.

"Okay, I am scared," I looked at Harmony and said. "Me too," Harmony said.

Neither one of us said another word as we watched the fire pop and crackle in front of us. I took her hand in mine, and she laid her head on my shoulder. I just kept thinking that just a few days ago, we had not even met, and now our lives were so entwined I couldn't get away from her if I wanted to. This seemed so natural and right that I had no thoughts of leaving anyway. After a while, I realized I needed to go home to bed because I had to be at work at 7:00 a.m. I told Harmony I needed to go home to sleep, and she kissed me, and I headed home.

The next day was Thursday, so when I got to work, I found my boss and got Friday off. The whole day seemed to drag on and on. At first, I thought it was because I really didn't want to go tomorrow on this wild-goose chase, and then it hit me that the reason the day was going so slow was because I was looking forward to being with Harmony on this adventure.

When I got home, I quickly showered and changed clothes and drove over to Pearl's to see Harmony. She was sitting on the porch with the fallen angels, and when she saw me drive up, I saw her smile from ear to ear. I came over and sat next to her, and she jumped up and sat on my lap as everyone smiled at me and her. I am sure they all knew we were falling in love, and so did I. She kissed me and made small talk, but she couldn't stay still on my lap, and so I asked her to go for a walk with me.

We headed off toward the river, and when we got there, we found a gravel bar and took our shoes off and waded to it and sat down.

She looked into my eyes and asked, "What do you think about this trip?"

I replied, "I think I am scared but think it will be an adventure of a lifetime."

She took my hand, and we just sat and talked about the trip. We discussed what clothes we were going to take, what food we might need to take, who was going to drive first, and where we might stop to eat lunch. I told her I wanted to stop for a little bit to see my parents and introduce her to them. I saw a loving smile come over her face when I told her that. After a while, we got up and headed back to the house to eat supper.

After supper, we again settled down into the living room and talked about everything but the trip. When it was getting late, we decided on the time to meet, and I said my goodbyes and went on home to sleep.

Sleep! That didn't happen much that night. I tossed and turned and seemed to beat up my pillow and blankets all night. I am sure I slept some, but not enough to feel good in the morning.

In the morning, I threw some things in a bag and started toward Harmony's house to pick her up. I saw Charles walking to his car and stopped to say bye. I didn't realize at the time that I would not be seeing him for quite a while. When I got to the house, Harmony was standing on the front porch with her bag and an old-fashioned picnic basket. It was so cute. It looked like we were just heading to the beach.

After we got everything loaded, we slipped into the house and talked to her parents for a minute, and then something happened that really shook me. Pearl asked us to bow our heads, and she led us in a prayer. It kind of made me shiver all over and realize Pearl was taking this more seriously than Harmony and I were. Maybe I should get in the spirit of what lay ahead of us.

When Harmony and I got into the little Bug, we said goodbye, and off we went. Neither of us talked for some time. I am sure we were both thinking about Pearl and her prayer. Finally, I couldn't not stand it anymore, and I talked about small things to Harmony. She seemed to be relieved too, and so the first part of the trip went fine. When we got to my parents' house, I brought her into the house and found my parents sitting at the kitchen table just finished with their breakfast.

When they saw Harmony, they both lit like a Christmas tree. We sat down with them, and we talked.

Mother started with, "You are such a pretty young woman. Where are you from?"

Harmony answered her question. Then it was Father's turn. "Harmony, we have met your mother, and I can see that you favor her. You are as pretty as she is, and you have her hair and her eyes. How tall are you?"

Harmony answered all their questions and asked where she might find the bathroom. When she was gone, it was my turn to answer questions.

"We knew you met Pearl down there and you told about her daughter, but we didn't realize she would be so beautiful," my mother said.

I smiled.

Father just smiled and said, "You look very happy. As happy as we have seen you in months."

I knew what they were saying, and I had to agree with them. After Sam's death, I didn't even want to talk to a woman, let alone fall in love with one.

Harmony came back to the table, and we all talked for a while and then moved into the living room. I told them we were going to Chicago to pick up some things, and I thought it would be a good idea to have Sam's parents meet Harmony. I wanted it all to be aboveboard with them too. My parents said that they thought that would be best, but I could see the horror in both of their faces when I said I was going to introduce Harmony to Sam's parents.

By the way, I was never going to do that anyway. I just told them that so we had an excuse to be going to Chicago. That was another thing Pearl had schooled us on: never tell anyone else what your true motive is for going to Chicago.

After we left my parents' house, we drove in silence to the interstate and took it north toward Des Moines. It was a great fall day, and the trees were turning all different colors, so I just looked out the window at the forest as we drove and marveled at God's work. I was also trying to keep mind off the work at hand and the chance that I would never see this area again. But when I looked at Harmony, I realized there are still things in my life that are good enough to fight for.

When we got closer to Des Moines, I realized that we were being followed by an ugly green car. I don't know how long it had been following me, but I could see it now. I told Harmony, and we quickly made a plan to find out for sure if it was indeed following us or if I was just paranoid. I found a gas station, and as I waited in the car, Harmony acted like she was stopping to use the restroom. When she went into the store, the car kept driving away like they were going on. I felt so much better as she got back into the car. I could see it in her face too as we drove back on the interstate.

We were almost out of the Des Moines when I looked in the mirror to see that same ugly green car slip behind us as we drove. I thought a minute and then told Harmony, "My sister lives just about five miles from here, and I think we should go there because I have a plan that I think will work for us." I got off the highway and drove straight to my sister's house.

When we got there, we drove right into the drive and got out and headed to the front door. I knew they were already gone to work, but I rang the doorbell anyway to see if anybody was home. In the meantime, we watched out of the corner of our eyes as the green car drove by the house and went down the road. When it was out of sight, I grabbed the spare key from the hiding place my sister had showed me and opened the door and put it back where it was.

The plan was simple: as soon as we saw the car was parked down the block, Harmony would get into the car and head down to the grocery store and park and go in, leaving the car unlocked. I would wait for five minutes after she was gone and slip out the back door down to a walk path that I had walked before. It would take me sight unseen right to the grocery store, and I would get into the car and wait for Harmony to come out, and we could be back on the highway in five minutes.

We watched as the green car parked down the block, and then I kissed Harmony as she left to drive off. When she drove off, the ugly green car stayed where it was. I waited for five minutes and slipped out the back door and onto the path. It was such a nice fall day I took my time walking. The trees were so beautiful, and the air was so fresh that I just about forgot what I was doing as I strolled along with not a care in the world, then it hit me, and I picked up the pace until I could see the parking lot and the yellow Beetle standing like a sore thumb. It took about seven or eight minutes for me to walk to the car in the parking lot, and then I was into the car. Harmony was watching from the store, and when she saw me, she walked quickly to the car, and we drove off.

The interstate was quiet as we drove along toward the Illinois border. We would be in Illinois soon and about seven hours from Chicago. We were making great time, and if this was all the problems we encountered, we would be home and safe faster than we ever thought.

Harmony spoke, "Why don't we find a place to stop and eat? My mother packed us enough food to feed a small town so we should be considerate enough to eat some of it."

"That's a good idea. Look for somewhere we can get off the road and not be seen," I replied.

We drove farther than we wanted because it didn't seem that we could find any place like that as we drove. Finally, the bridge came into sight that we needed to cross the Mississippi River, and we could see a road that would take us right to the river if we could get off the interstate soon. The exit came, and we took it toward the road we had seen from the interstate. When we got to it, we found it was just a dirt road that ran along the river for fishermen to stop and put their boats in the river.

I drove into a bank of trees that would hide us from the interstate and any prying eyes. The trees were cottonwood trees, and this time of year, they were releasing their leaves into the air, and they were blowing in the wind to parts unknown. It was a great sight to see when we stopped and opened the doors, we could grab the leaves as they came toward the ground. Some drifted toward the ground, but most were taken up into the air on the breeze and sped toward their destination.

Cottonwoods grew as high as 150 feet along this river, and several would be a much as one hundred years old. Since they like to stay where there is a lot of water for them to drink, they often fall over because of the sandy soil and water in the soil. But they are very regal trees with leaves that rustle as the wind runs through them. I couldn't have picked a better spot for a picnic with a pretty lady if I had to.

We first walked in the trees hand and hand toward the river and found an old log from a tree that had fallen years ago. I spread the blanket, and Harmony put the picnic basket on the blanket, and we went to the water's edge. From bank to bank, it was about a quarter mile across. Not as wide as most places on the Old Muddy, but it was still impressive to see, smell, and hear the sounds it made as it made its way toward the gulf.

When I looked at Harmony, she had a little glint in her eye that I really didn't like as we stood holding hands. We went back to the blanket in the shade of the trees and sat down.

"David, what are you thinking about me when you look at me when we are holding hands on this river?" she said.

I played coy and said, "What are you talking about, Harmony?" She looked away, and I felt badly for making her have to look away, so I said, "My heart tells me that I am falling in love with you, but after what happened in the past, my head tells me to take it easy and go slow."

She turned toward me and was smiling, giving me a kiss, and hugged me so hard I thought I was going to break. "David, I feel the same way as you do. I haven't had much luck with boys in the past because they were immature and only want to feel my boobs and slobber on me. I see that you are not like that, and I feel free to talk to you without you groping me and make me do things I don't want to do. When you kiss me, I feel like the top of my head will explode, and my heart flutters when you touch me. I think we should make love here on this blanket. What do you think?"

Whoa, that one threw me for a loop, and I was speechless. It was very awkward for a minute as the silence took over. I knew I should say something fast, but I wanted the words to be comforting for her, and also I wanted to let her know I was honored she asked me but confused as to what to do from here.

So I took my time to answer. I did take her hand and look in her eyes as I thought of the words I would say.

"Harmony, I think that is a great idea." She laughed and hugged me again. Then she started to kiss me and take her shirt off at the same time. I took her hands and pulled her shirt back down and looked her right in the eyes as I said, "But not here and not like this. I want it to be special for you and me. I want us to do it right. We need to be married before we do anything like this. I know you will agree that it would be great doing it here, but I think you would feel different after we get done, and I want it to be the best day of our lives. Don't you agree?"

She had this funny look on her face as I said these words to her, but I could also see in her face that she knew I was right. I quickly grabbed her and kissed her and pushed her onto her back with me coming to rest on top of her, saying, "I never thought I would find another woman to love as much I loved Samantha until I met you. I want us to do this right so we will be together forever with no regrets and no unanswered questions between us."

Harmony smiled and said, "You are a good man, David Hunter. I concur with your thinking." Man, what a weight was lifted off my heart when she said that.

Harmony got up and got the picnic basket then spread the food out on the blanket. Her mother had outdone herself with the food she packed. There was a bottle of red wine, cold chicken, potato salad, pork and beans, toasted garlic bread, and for dessert, homemade chocolate cookies. We ate, talked, and laughed for the next hour before we lay down in each other's arms and drifted off to sleep. It was the middle of the day when we woke up and got everything back into the car. I drove the car back onto the highway and across the bridge into Illinois toward Chicago. We had not driven long when I saw a police car come up behind us and turn on his flashing lights. I turned toward Harmony and said, "Be watchful because I was doing the speed limit. It might be a trick. If there is trouble, remember to meet me at the nearest church."

Harmony looked worried and said, "Be careful if they put you in the car. I will be all right, so don't worry about me."

I pulled over to the side of the interstate and watched as the state police pulled behind me. The first thing I noticed as both policemen got out of the car was the Iowa State Police sign on the door; this was Illinois. The second thing I noticed was, their uniforms were both too small for them, and I told Harmony about these facts. One policeman came to each side of the car, and I rolled my window down.

"Something wrong, Officer?" I asked to the one at my window.

He replied, "You were speeding when you went down the last hill, son. Would you give me your license and step out of the car?" I complied and stepped out of the car. "Will you step into the patrol car so I can run your license?" he said.

I was thinking all the time we walked to the car, and I was opening the door. I put my hand on the door with one hand and, with the other, pulled my amulet off and wadded it into a ball in my hand as I stepped into the passenger side and closed the door. I looked out the windshield as the other officer ordered Harmony out of the car and had her put her hands on top of the car. He made her spread her legs and was running his hands up and down her legs then went on up her back to her front and grabbed her boobs.

I looked over at the officer in the car with me, and he was watching the scene out the windshield instead of watching what I was doing. He had his mouth open, and he was dripping saliva down the front of his uniform. In one move, I took my amulet and popped it into his mouth. He turned toward me, and nothing happened for a few seconds, then he was gone, poof. There was a sound like little pieces of glass hitting the seat where he had been sitting along with all the clothes he had on sitting in the seat and floor.

I looked at the seat, and there was my amulet, along with the service pistol he had on. I grabbed both of them and bolted out the door toward Harmony and the other officer. He was having so much fun groping Harmony that he never knew I was there until I hit him with the gun as hard as I could on the back of his head. It was a sound like when you thump a ripe watermelon, then he went limp and dropped like a sack of potatoes. I still had my amulet in my hand, so I just dropped it on top of his back. The same sound I heard in the police car like little pieces of glass came from the body, and then it was gone too.

Harmony had dropped to her knees when I hit the ghoul, and she was still in that position when I helped her up and into the car. I quickly turned and ran back to the police car, wiping my prints off the gun as I ran. I opened the door on the passenger side and put the gun back in the holster on the driver's seat. Then, I quickly wiped everywhere I had touched in the car, and just before I closed the door, I reached into the back seat and grabbed a ziplock bag that was sitting there. When I got back to our car, I opened the front trunk and threw the bag in and closed the lid.

Harmony was in shock and was shivering uncontrollably when I got into the car. I took our heavy coats from the back seat and wrapped her up in them and gave her a pillow to put her head on. I brushed the hair off her face and saw she was as white as a sheet. I drove to the next exit and turned off the main road onto a gravel road. About a mile down the road, I saw an old barn, and I drove to that and drove the car around the back of the barn so no one could see us.

As quickly as I could, I got the blanket out of the trunk and our bags of clothing. I lay the blanket down in the shade of an old elm tree and positioned the bags on the blanket. Then, opening the passenger door up, I picked Harmony up and carried her to the blanket. Putting her head down gently then her legs, I put the bags under her legs and elevated her legs above her head. I ran back to the car and grabbed the coats and put them around her then lay next to her with my arm over her.

As I watched her, the color started to come back to her face little by little, and I knew she would be okay. She must have been overwhelmed when that creature started to grope her, and it made her body and mind shut down. It must have been like being raped for her. I had heard about women being raped, and during the rape, their mind and body would shut down. Some women would not let a man touch them for a long time after that. I hoped and prayed that would not be the case with Harmony.

After about an hour, Harmony started to stir under the coats, and she threw them off and sat up suddenly. She saw me and grabbed me and started to cry. I just held her until she was done crying and then took her face in my hands and looked into her eyes.

"Are you feeling better?" I asked.

She shook her head and said, "How did we get here?"

"What do you remember about what happened?" I asked her.

She thought for a moment and said, "Nothing, I just remember a police car stopping us and an officer at your window asking you to step out of the car. What did happen after that?"

I didn't know if I should tell her, but if we were going to face these demons again, she needed to know, and I needed to know I could count on her. The best thing to do was to tell her everything and see if that would instill enough hate in her to act first and then think later. So I told her the whole story, and I watched her face as I told her. There it was; I could see it in her eyes as I recounted to her what had happened. She jumped up and ran to the tree, and I thought she was going to hit it with her fist, but she just smacked it with her hand.

After she had calmed down, we put everything back in the car and headed back to the interstate. As we were getting on the highway, she turned to me and said, "David, I am so sorry that I was not more help to you fighting these demons off. I feel helpless. I hope this will not happen again, or we might end up dead."

I looked at her and said, "I don't think that will happen again. What do you feel when you think about that guy putting his hands all over?"

Her whole body shook with disgust, and then her face got redder and redder as she thought about it. "I will be ready next time, and they will never lay their nasty hands on me again," she said. I smiled and knew she would be much more alert in the future.

Harmony turned on the radio, and the news was on. She was just about to change the channel when we heard they were looking for two men who stole a police car in Iowa and were last seen heading toward the Illinois border in it. They also said the two men had broken into a house just outside Des Moines,. When the police confronted them in the house, they had subdued the police and had taken their uniforms and car. We looked at each other and laughed when we thought about the police finding the car and the clothes but no bodies.

Harmony turned the station to music and started to sing along with the radio as we drove toward Chicago. But my thoughts were somewhere else because of what we had gotten ourselves into. I was worried not just for Harmony but for myself as well. Then it occurred to me that we had an ace in the hole, God. If it was his will, then we would be okay, and if not, well, I would talk to him about that when I see him.

When we got close to Chicago, Harmony got out the map that her mother had drawn for us. I never did like this town, and today was no exception. Before, when I would come for a visit with Sam, we would drive the trip after we had worked all night. When we got here, I was so turned around that the whole time we were here, I was lost and could not get my bearings. It must be the way we would go to the east side of Chicago to end up on the north side. It made no sense to me, but the map was complete, and we had no problem with the directions.

We pulled up to a brownstone building that looked to me there were about thirty floors in it. Just before we got out of the car, I took Harmony's hand as she was trying to get out and pulled her back inside the car. She shut the door and turned to me as to say "What do you want?" I pulled her close and gave her a long kiss and then opened my door and ran around to open hers.

I took her hand, and we started toward the front door. Harmony looked at the directions her mother had given her and pushed the buzzer by the name Karl Freeman, which her mother had written. Nothing! We waited for a minute, and then she pushed it again, and still nothing.

"Now what do we do?" I asked.

Harmony looked at me and then at the directions then pushed the buzzer once more.

A man's voice answered this time, "What do you want?" He seemed pleasant enough.

Harmony put her face close to the speaker and said, "My name is Harmony, and I have come because my mother has asked me to come to speak to Karl Freeman. My mother's name is Pearl."

The man's voice came back on the speaker and said, "I don't know you or your mother, and I don't know what you are talking about."

I stepped up to the speaker and said, "My name is David Hunter, and I came with Harmony to see you and speak to you."

There was a long pause, and then the voice came on again, "Where were you born, what is your mother's maiden name, what is your social security number, what is your address, and what is your grandmother's name?" I answered all these questions, then he came back on and told us the apartment number, buzzed us in, and we went right in.

We stepped through another door, and it opened into a lobby with floors and ceilings made up of small tiles that were black and white. The walls were painted white, and there were two more entrances on the right and left of the lobby. Ahead of us was a bank of elevators, and we proceeded to them. I held the door open for Harmony, and we hit the button, and we were off toward the thirtieth floor. Suddenly, I felt light-headed as we assented up toward our floor. We stopped, and the doors opened, and we were on solid ground again.

I looked down the hallway and found the right door and knocked. The door opened, and a man in his late years, with average height and build, was looking back at us. He was dressed well with slacks and a white shirt and had slippers on. I noticed he had a gold watch on one wrist, and on the other was a nice gold chain. He wore a wedding ring, but there was no evidence anybody else was living there.

The door opened into the living room, and across from the front door was a big window overlooking the street. There was a hallway to the right of the front door, and I could see there was a kitchen at the end of the hallway. There were two more doors in the hallway, and they were both shut. To the left of the front door on the far wall was two more doors at each end of the wall. They were closed also.

As we walked into the middle of the living room, I could see the wall on the right, and it had pictures of people from the top half up almost to the ceiling. I stopped to look at the pictures as Harmony was seated by Karl, and then he turned toward me and saw that I was looking at his pictures.

The words came like a warm breeze as he spoke, "They are all dead but me."

I turned and looked at him and then back toward the wall of pictures. "All?" I asked.

"Yes, I have outlived them all—my wife, my children, my grandchildren, my great-grandchildren, and all my friends."

I turned toward him, and he motioned me toward a chair. "If I may ask, how old are you?"

He looked out the window for a long time, and then a smile came to his face, and he said, "Older than dirt." He laughed out loud, and we both laughed with him. But I could see the pain in his face as he ended his laugh and sat down in a chair between both of us. He continued, "So now I am going home to see my family, and you are here to help me go. I have waited for this day for so many years, you wouldn't believe me if I told you how many years I have waited."

Karl asked me the same questions he had asked when we rang his buzzer and excused himself. He went to the door at the far end of the wall, the one closest to the window, opened it, and went in, closing the door as he went, leaving Harmony and me to look around the room and talk. I thought he was just going to get the crystals, but he was in there at least ten minutes, so after a while, I got up and looked at the pictures again. Part of them were older than 1901, and they ranged clear up to the 1960s. I guessed then they quit. Several of them were men and women around the Civil War, because I recognized the uniforms they wore. Several were of women around the same era also.

I returned to my seat, wondering out loud why the pictures had stopped around the sixties. We both were thinking about it when Karl returned to us and sat down with a small bag in his hand. He handed a red velvet bag to me and motioned me to open it. I opened it and let the contents spill onto my hand. They were beautiful. Diamonds of all colors and sizes spilled into my hand. They all were translucent, and I could see my hand right through them.

Karl took the stones and put them back into the bag and said, "This is what you have driven all this way for."

"Okay, I give up. What are they besides diamonds?" I asked.

He looked at the bag with a smile and said, "I asked that very question in 1860 just before the Civil War was starting." That meant he was over 120 years old. We both looked at him and then at the pictures on the wall and back to him. He just nodded his head in agreement of the unasked question we both wanted to ask.

He began, "These crystals have the names of all the people in this region who are alive and died who are saved through Christ. This is the Book of Names the Bible talks about, and it changes every minute of every day until Christ comes back to earth. These are God's souls that have been amassing in the last several hundred years in this region. There are many regions in the world, and each of them has a book of names.

"When Satan was thrown out of heaven with his followers, he was thrown down to earth to wander until the last days when Christ comes back. He controls these regions and has a prince over each of them. That prince will know everything that goes on in his region, so as soon as you leave here, he will know and will unleash his demons on you to get this bag for his master. This is what you have been sent here to get and return to the next person for safekeeping until the day Christ returns to earth."

He continued, "Let me tell you about these crystals. If Satan has his way, he will steal these crystals from you as you take it back home. He will spare nothing to get these crystals, because if he gets them, these names will be his and these souls too. He will send his minions out to hunt you down, kill you, and take the crystals. So, make no mistake, as long as you have these stones, your lives will be in danger."

I asked, "Then why hasn't Satan come and taken the stones from you?"

The man replied, "This is hallowed ground, and Satan and none of his demons can cross onto hallowed ground. So, if you get into any trouble, go to the nearest church and consult whoever is in charge. You will be safe there until you leave the church grounds." These were the same words Harmony's mother had spoken to us before we left.

I continued my questions, "I saw in movies Satan can come into the church and take anybody out of them. Are you telling the truth that we will be safe in the church if we go in?"

"Yes," the old man replied. He added, "You can kill the demons with holy water sprayed on them and the amulet you wear on your neck. And in extreme cases, God will send his angels to do battle for you, so an angel can kill a demon also." From the fallen angels I had met at Harmony's house, I also knew they may be hurt or killed also. He continued, "Now I am old, tired and want to go home. I want you to stay for a while, and then when you are rested, come into my study and take the envelopes I have prepared on the desk and mail for me, please." He got up and started toward the door closest to the front door and then turned to face us and said, "Please, no matter what you hear or see, do not open this door until you feel it is safe."

Then he went in the door and shut it behind him.

Harmony jumped up and came to sit on the arm of my chair with a funny look on her face. She looked as if she had seen a ghost. She looked at me and said, "You know he is going in there to die, don't you?"

"No," I said. "Why do you think that?"

"I have heard about this before from my mother, and no matter what we see and hear, just like the man said, don't run and go into that room. He is going to be Raptured. You know when God takes a being to heaven without him first dying." I had read about it in the Bible but never thought I would be a witness.

All at once, there was a great light that seemed to come from every pore in the door the man had gone through. It came under the door and through the cracks around the door and even through the keyhole of the door. And with the light came great heat as if someone had opened a door of a furnace. It lasted just a few minutes, maybe just seconds, then it was gone.

I jumped up and tried to run to the door, but Harmony was on me in a flash, pulling me down toward the floor, and then she was on top of me with all her weight, pinning me to the floor. Just as fast as she had fallen on top of me, she was up and helping me to my feet. I could only look at her and wonder what was going on behind that door and where she got all that strength to do that.

She guided me back to the my chair and then went to a little bar near the corner and found two glasses and some whiskey then returned back to me. She gave me both glasses and poured a healthy drink in both glasses then put the bottle back and returned to me. She raised her glass and clinked it on mine and swallowed the thing in one gulp. I looked at her and then at the glass and did the same thing.

There was a smell in the air I had smelled when I was younger. It was burning flesh, hair, and clothes. When I was young, there was a fire at a house where a woman was burned to death, and that was the same smell I smelled when I went with my father to look at the ruins.

It had been about five minutes after the flash of light and heat, and Harmony stood up and started toward the door Karl had entered, and I quickly followed her. She tried the handle, and it was cold, so she opened the door, and we left it open as we entered a bedroom. There was a big four-poster bed against one wall, a dresser right in front of the bed on another wall, a big window like the one in the living room on another wall, and on the last wall was a nice wingback chair with a footstool that matched it. On the chair, there was a charred spot about the size of the cushion, and on the floor in front of the chair, the char continued there. Nothing else was burned—not the chair, the rug, or the footstool, just that spot.

I turned to Harmony and asked, "Where is Karl?"

Harmony looked around the room and said, "Karl is gone, and I think I know what happened to him. He has been Raptured."

"That sounds reasonable to me," I said.

Harmony continued, "It is so much friction it starts a fire so hot the body is burned up in less than one-hundredth of a second. The reason nothing else burns up is, it happens so fast that nothing else is touched."

"I think the scientist call this Spontaneous Combustion," I said. Later, when I went back to work at the university, I researched spontaneous combustion at the library and found that since there has been records kept, about two hundred confirmed cases have been recorded. One article I read said they think this has been going on since the beginning of time. That would mean thousands of cases.

Science has never been able to explain what makes this happen.

Harmony and I left the room just as we found it. We wiped all finger-prints off, cleaned the glasses, put them away, and headed toward the other door Karl had gone in to retrieve the letters he had told us to mail for him.

We entered this door and saw a big old desk right in the middle of the room. There was a big bookshelf behind it that took up the whole back wall clear to the ceiling. We retrieved the envelopes lying on the desk and exited the same way as we entered, making sure to clean the door handle.

We went to the front door and went out the apartment, making sure to wipe everything off. We entered the elevator and went to the lobby and out the front door. Nobody saw us, and we saw no one. When we were out the front door, we looked around and found a blue box for the mail and put them in.

When we got into the car, we just sat there for a while and didn't say anything to each other. I started the car and took off, with neither of us saying a word for about ten minutes or so. I finally turned down a quiet street and pulled the car up under a big maple tree and turned the engine off.

Turning to Harmony, I said, "What just happened in that apartment? Did we just witness a miracle?" At that, Harmony just shook her head yes.

I started the car and turned around in the road so we could go back the way we had come. I found the on-ramp and headed west toward Des Moines and home. The sun was beginning to set when we stopped to go to the bathroom. Why hadn't we gone to the bathroom at Karl's? We decided that one person would stay in the car with the bag and the other would go to the bathroom, then we would switch. Harmony would go first and then me.

When it was my turn, I hopped out of the car and ran into the bathroom. After I was done, I washed my hands and stepped out of the door. The night air was going colder just after the sun had set, and I filled my lungs with the cool, crisp air before starting to the car. That was when I saw them coming toward the car. Two men dressed in black and ugly as sin. I just had time to yell at Harmony as they reached the car. She quickly locked the doors and started the car. She backed right over one of them and started toward the on-ramp with this joker right behind her on foot. All of a sudden, she hit the brakes and rammed the little car in reverse and hit the guy so hard he flew over the car and hit right in front of it.

I ran toward the car, and when I got to the passenger door, she had opened it, and I hopped in and slammed the door shut. Out of the corner of my eye, I saw the other man who had been run over grab my door and start to open it. I took my foot and forced the door open real fast, and he was flung to the curb, then I grabbed the handle and closed it just as Harmony hit the other man that was lying in front of the car. This little car drove right up his ass and right off his head with a crunch. Harmony shifted gears, and off we went.

I looked back as she shifted again and entered the highway. I was sure that one guy was dead and the other one was wounded badly. I turned around, saying, "Way to go, Harmony." She smiled and drove on.

We had not gone five miles when a car drove up beside us, and I could see the same guy I had kicked off the door driving it. Harmony saw him at the same time I had. She turned the wheel away from the car just as it was going to hit us, and then she slammed on the brakes so hard it nearly threw me out the windshield. Back then, nobody had seat belts on. The little car headed off the road toward an outer road, and when we hit it, she turned the car in the other direction and headed down the outer road the wrong way.

There were cars coming toward us, and she was swerving to miss them and still keeping the car on the road. I looked in the back window, and the other car was still keeping up with us. When she saw a chance, she turned off this road onto another one that took us down a residential area. We were lost but finally slipped the guy behind us.

We wandered around the side streets until we decided to stop and ask directions to get back on the highway. We looked around and found not one gas station but finally found a big old Catholic church with lights shining out in front. We decided to stop and see if there was anyone in the church who could help us. Harmony stopped and parked the car and gave me the bag to put it in my pocket. We got out and ran toward the church.

I grabbed the door of the church and swung it open for Harmony to enter, and I followed her inside. There was a big open sanctuary with pews from the back to the front on each side of the room and an aisle in the middle leading from the back to the pulpit in front. As we walked toward the front, I marveled at the stained glass pictures that made up the windows. It was something you see in a picture. As we neared the front, I could see several people in the pews nearest the front who were sitting and praying with their heads bowed.

Out of the corner my eye, I saw a figure moving along the outside aisle to my left, and I could see that it was probably the priest because of the way he was dressed. When we turned toward that figure, Harmony took my hand and said, "Just ask him the way back to the highway and no more." I looked at her and nodded my head in agreement. We approached the priest, and I asked the question. He gave us the directions we were looking for, and we started toward the door and out.

When I swung the door open to let Harmony out, she stopped short, and I actually ran into her from behind. I looked over her shoulder to see what had made her stop so short, and there they were. Five men standing on the sidewalk between us and our car. At this time, I grabbed Harmony by the hand and pulled her back inside the church before closing the door.

I looked at her, and we both said, at the same time, "What are we going to do?" She was thinking I had an answer, and I was thinking she would have one. We regrouped and slid into a seat next to the door.

My first thought was to run to the back of the church to see if there was another door there that we might get out. So I grabbed her hand, telling her as we walked what I wanted to do. As we neared the side of the church to go to the back, we came face-to-face with the same priest.

"Was there something else I can do for you?" the priest asked as we almost ran over him.

I looked at Harmony and then at the priest and said, "Yes, there is. There are some men that are out front waiting for us to leave so they can harm us."

The priest said, "Well, then, let's call the police and see what they want."

"No, they are not the kind of men that would care what the police would say. They would just kill them and then kill us too. You, too, if you get in their way," Harmony replied.

I decided to take the priest into our confidence and tell him what he needed to know to help us. "Please don't ask us a lot of questions, but we are on a mission for God, and we need your help." The priest looked us both over and asked, "A mission for God?" "Yes. We are carrying something that belongs to God, and these men will stop at nothing to get it from us. It is a matter of hundreds of souls that would be lost if they get it from us," Harmony said.

I looked at the priest, and I could see he was not convinced about our story, but he started to lead us back into the back of the church toward the back door. He started to open it, and I stopped him, saying, "Is there any way you can look outside without being seen or opening the door?"

"Yes," he said. "There is a window above us on the next floor that looks over the back door. I will go and see and then come back to tell you." After that, he went and came back in about two minutes.

When he came back, he said, "There are five guys just out the back door, and they look like they have hate in their eyes for you."

I sat down on the floor to think, and Harmony and the priest stood over me, waiting for me to say something. When I got up, I asked the priest, "Do you have holy water here?" He said he did, and he directed me to it. I then asked, "Is there something we could use to take some of it with us?" Again, he said yes.

The priest led us to the basement, and there was a kitchen, a snack machine, and a pop machine in one corner of the basement. He went into the kitchen and brought a jar with a lid out. As he was doing that, I spied something else that I thought would do a better job. Beside the pop machine was a box for the empty bottles to be put in. I took one of them and then checked my pockets for change. The machine took twenty-five cents for a bottle of pop, and I needed two bottles. I had seventy-five cents, so I bought two bottles of Coke and took a drink of one and asked Harmony to do the same.

We ran up to the main floor and filled the other bottle with holy water. We finished filling the other two bottles, with Coke in them, to the top with holy water and headed back to the back door. I told Harmony the plan and told her to follow my lead but not do anything until I said so. She agreed. We thanked the priest and then headed toward the door.

The priest opened the door for us, and I was sure he was still watching us as we stepped out to meet the guys. Five men were standing just below the two steps to the alley, and they looked mean as hell. No pun intended.

I sized them up as we walked to the top of the steps. The leader was a tall person with a trench coat on that hung almost to the top of his boots. He was dressed all in black like all the other demons I had encountered before him, not! He had long greasy hair and a face that even his mother could not love. I looked to see what part of his body was deformed, and as I looked from head to toe, I almost laughed out loud. As I ran my eyes down to his feet, there it was. One of his boots had been cut halfway up from the toe to reveal his toes sticking out of it. His foot was half again the size as the other.

There were three guys all in a row beside him, and I could see another one hunkering down in the back. I knew I could get the four in front of me with one motion, but the fifth man I could not. I hoped that Harmony would be able to get him when the time came.

The leader started to step toward us, and Harmony and I took a step backward toward the back door. When he stopped and looked at us, that was when I let them have it. I put my thumb on the opening and shook up the bottle of Coke I had in my hand and sprayed all four men on the front row. The leader lunged toward me, and before he could grab me, he was gone with only the sound of little pieces of glass hitting the concrete. The other three disappeared the same way. Left standing by himself was the one in the back. He stood taller and started coming toward us, saying, "Don't spray me. I am here to help you." Harmony didn't even hesitate as she shook up her bottle and sprayed him from head to toe. He had such a look of amazement on his face when she did that, but nothing happened. He was still there, dripping Coke from his head to his feet.

He wiped the Coke from his eyes, and again, he said, "I have been sent to help you get out of here and back home." He continued, "My name is Mica Tacoha Accesh, but you can call me Mica."

"So, you say you have been sent to help us. Does that mean you are an angel from God?" I asked. I felt a hand on my shoulder and quickly turned to see the priest looking at us in amazement. He walked toward Mica and touched him on the arm and looked at where the other four men had been standing and then turned and went back inside the church. Not a word came out of his mouth. I figured he was in shock.

Mica asked, "What was that demon brew you used to kill those demons with?"

I looked at Harmony, and we both laughed at the same time. "It was Coke and holy water. We took a little Coke out of the bottle and filled it up with holy water. When you shake it up, it explodes and sprays all over."

Mica put his finger to his mouth and tasted it. He smiled and said, "It is good. I have not been on earth before, so you must teach me what to say and do so I may fit in." Both Harmony and I smiled at our newfound friend.

We quickly exited the alley and quietly got to the car. The other demons were still out front of the church watching the door. I asked Mica what car they were in, and he said he had no clue. We slipped behind them and put the car in neutral and pushed it around the corner before we got in. We had to put Mica in the back, and with his tall build, he looked like a clown in one of those clown cars.

As we drove toward the Iowa border, we talked about what we needed to do to keep these demons off our trail, and one thing seemed certain. We needed to get rid of this yellow car and find something different. I was against this idea because this had been my wife's car. I loved this car, but I also knew it stuck out like a sore thumb, so in the end, I agreed to get rid of it.

It was about 9:00 p.m. at night, and I realized we had nothing to eat since lunch, and I was getting hungry. I asked if anyone else was getting hungry, and Mica looked at me as if he really didn't have a clue. So Harmony explained what hunger was and how he needed to eat to keep the body he was in going. Mica agreed he needed to eat too, and we told him we would tell him when to eat until he caught on to the schedule of eating. Who was going to tell him about going to the bathroom?

We pulled off the highway into a McDonald's and got out of the car. When we did, Mica started toward the front door with us and then turned around and headed back toward the car. We were curious about what he was doing, so we followed him back to the car. He stood there for a minute and started sniffing all around the car until he got to the trunk, which was in the front of the car. He asked me what was in there, and I said, "Just clothes and a spare tire." He then asked me if he could see into it. I popped the trunk lid, and then I could smell what he was smelling.

"What is that smell?" Harmony asked.

I was embarrassed but said, "When I got into the patrol car, I smelled it and realized it was the demon's lunch. I thought it might come in handy, so I went back and got it and threw it in the trunk."

Mica smiled and said, "That is the way they have been tracking us. They know every place we have been and the direction we are driving because of that smell. They can smell this for fifty miles if the wind is right. Get rid of it."

I grabbed the bag and took it to the trash and threw it in. Harmony asked, "What was it anyway?"

I said, "I think it was my sister's trash because that is where they got the police car. I didn't look in it but think it might be dirty diapers and spoiled meat."

Harmony held her nose and ran toward the door to get away from the smell.

When we got to the counter, we both tried to teach Mica about the menu and what might be in the food he was going to eat. We got him a Big Mac, fries, and a large chocolate shake.

I decided to have some fun with Mica because he said he had never tried to eat anything. So when his food came, we showed him how to eat the sandwich and the fries and got him a straw for the shake. When it came time to show him how to suck the liquid from the straw, he did real well and was very impressed with the liquid and how cold it was. He never knew cold. This is when I played the trick on him. I told him that if he drank the shake real quick through the straw, he could get the whole effect of the shake.

When I told him that, I winked at Harmony to let her know the joke was on. Mica saw the wink and asked, "What was that?"

I said, "What was what?"

He said, "When you turned your head towards Harmony and closed and opened your eye real quick."

I smiled and said, "I don't know what you are talking about," then went back to eating my sandwich.

We both watched as Mica took the shake and started to quickly drink the cold liquid through the straw. He must have drunk about a quarter of it when, all of a sudden, he put the drink down and started putting his hands to his head in pain then passed out onto the floor. I knew he would have a "brain freeze" but didn't know it would make him pass out. We quickly grabbed him off the floor and set him down in his chair and put his head on the table. It was about thirty seconds before he moved, and then he vomited all over the table and onto the floor.

The manager came and asked if he was all right, and we told him he had just drunk his shake too fast. We explained to the manager that Mica was not from the US and never had a shake before. I told the manager we would clean it up, and we did, and then we ordered another meal for Mica. I told Mica I was sorry and explained to him what a "wink" meant. We told him we were just having fun with him. But I didn't think he was very pleased with us and didn't talk to us for a while. I didn't blame him.

After we got done eating, we all went to the bathroom, so I took Mica with me. He had never been in a bathroom, and I showed him the toilets and the urinals with a brief description of what each one was used for. I took him to the sink and showed him how to wash and dry his hands, and we were off.

When we got to the car, Harmony jumped into the back, and Mica rode up front with me. I knew he felt better because he could stretch his body out better in the front than the back seat. As we drove into Iowa, I was telling them about all the towns in Iowa that were named for great Indian chiefs. After several hours, we made it to Des Moines, where we would turn south for the last leg to Missouri and then home. Harmony needed to go to the bathroom, so I stopped at a gas station and filled up the car.

After I got gas, Mica and I went inside to get something drink. We sat around waiting for Harmony to get out of the bathroom, and after she didn't come out, I got worried and went to check on her. She was gone. No sign, no note, nothing. I rushed out to Mica and told him what had happened, and we both were thinking the same thing. The demons had gotten her and were wanting to trade for the stones. I was worried sick because of what had happened the first time we encountered the demons and what Harmony had endured that time.

Mica looked at me and said, "David, I think the best thing to do is keep driving towards your home and wait until the demons get in touch with us." I agreed and started off down the interstate toward Missouri.

I could not concentrate because of worrying about Harmony. I wished that Mica knew how to drive because I was so upset that I might have a wreck. Finally, I got my feelings under control, and we started to cruise down the road watching for any sign of Harmony, demons, or the car we had seen at the church. We went over and over what kind of car it had been, but we were having trouble about the color. I thought it was white, and Mica thought it had been dark blue. What a mess.

We were nearing Missouri, and no sign of anything when, out of the blue, we saw a figure alongside the road. He was standing next to a guardrail waiting for us. I slowed to a stop just in front of this tall, ugly demon.

We both jumped out, and I walked right up to him and put my face just inches from his nasty self. I could smell rotten food on his breath and see he was unclean. His teeth were almost green, his hair was greasy, his face was unwashed, clothes stank like pig shit, and I could smell his body order on top of everything else. The other thing I noticed was that one eye was almost twice the size of the other one. Eerie.

The first words out of his mouth were strange to me, but I realized Mica could understand him. He turned more toward Mica than me, and Mica talked to him in this strange language for several moments. The demon kept looking at me and then back to Mica, and I knew he would have tried to kill me if Mica was not there. Finally, Mica turned to me and led me back toward the car.

"He said they have Harmony and want to trade her for the stones, but I don't trust them. They will get the stones and then try to kill us all. They are not just walking away from this," Mica said. I agreed with him.

"What do you want to do then?" I asked.

"The only thing we can do is let them think we will trade and then try to free Harmony without getting killed in the process," he said. Again, I agreed with what he said. Mica walked back to the demon, and they talked for just a minute, then he came back to the car.

"Let's go," he said as he swung the car door open and got in.

When we got in the car and started down the road, Mica told me the directions to where they were wanting to trade. The demons wanted us to exit about a mile from here into a rest area that I knew well. Then we were to get out of our car and walk down the sidewalk toward a small lake and up the hill to a field house that overlooked the river.

I smiled and turned toward Mica, saying, "This is great. My grandfather used to own all this land, and I have played in these woods since I was a child. I know this area like the back of my hand, and we can lose them if we can get Harmony from them." I continued, "This is an old gravel pit where the lake is, and there are quartz crystals all over on the ground. We can switch the stones and put them in the bag instead of the diamonds. If they have never seen the rocks, they will not know the difference, then we can get away." Mica agreed, and we drove into the rest area and parked the car.

When we got out, I ran around to the passenger side and opened the door, got into the glove box, and got three things out. One was a flashlight, a small .38 pistol I had brought along for protection, and the other was the rest of the holy water Harmony had saved in a bottle from the church. We walked toward the lake, and I looked on the ground for the stones we needed to fool the demons. No luck. We stopped, so I could think, and then I got it.

When my brothers and sisters were young, we played around the lake when our parents brought us out here for picnics and camping. One thing we did was pick up the buckeyes from the trees and hide them in the old hollow trees. The other thing we picked up was the quartz, and we hid them in the hollows of the trees too. I looked around in the moonlight for a hollow tree and found one. I didn't want to shine my flashlight to tip the demons off, so I just put my hand in to feel for the stones. There was something there all right, but not what I was feeling for. It was a snake, and I took a stick and flipped him out of the tree.

Once again, I put my hand in and brought out buckeyes. Moving on to another tree, I did the same thing until I found one with the stones in it. I picked similar sizes and shapes and replaced all the diamonds with quartz. Then I put the diamonds into the hollow tree, and we started up the path toward the field house. It wasn't a field house; it was a sheltered picnic area with ten or so picnic tables on a concrete slab that overlooked a bluff toward the river.

This area brought back fond memories from my childhood: the times we spent camping and fishing at the lake and the river; coming here when the raspberries were ripe, picking them, canning the jelly, and storing it in the basement for long winter months with baked bread and jelly; Scout campouts, playing hide-and-seek in the woods, and the best of all, the hayrides in the fall with my friends and our girlfriends. This was the first place I kissed a girl.

Now this. Going up the hill to save the girl I loved with death and doom all around in the dark.

I turned to Mica and asked, "Can you see good in the dark?" "Yes, I can see good in the dark and can smell even better. They are watching us and listening to us as we come up the hill. There is one demon on each side of us and one behind us, and I think there is just one other holding Harmony at the top of the hill," he said.

As we got closer, I could see the two figures at the shelter and could make out Harmony standing beside one of the demons. All of a sudden, I felt scared, and Mica grabbed my arm and told me not to show any fear, or we would be dead. He told me they could smell fear just like an animal. So I thought back to when I was in the patrol car and how mad I was seeing something groping my girl. Now they had her again, and God only knows what they had been doing with her.

The others came up from behind us and slid around to the front to face us. Now all we would have to do is get Harmony from the demons, and we were home free. Mica started to move to the right, and I started to move to the left until they asked us to stop and give them the bag. I reached into my pocket and pulled out the bag and put it on the nearest picnic table so they could see it. I knew that this prize was worth more than all our lives, and so did the demons.

The one that had talked to us on the highway stepped forward with Harmony held tight in his hand. "You made a wise decision by bringing the stones here to trade for the girl," he said. Then he came closer, but I didn't want him to get too close, just close enough for me to throw some of this water on him.

"That is far enough," I said as I took a step toward them. "Now, let her go and you can get the stones."

"No, you throw the stones to me, and then I will let her go," he said.

"We can do this all night until the sun comes up," I said.

The demon eyed the bag and then looked to me. "Open the bag and pour the stones on the table." I did as he asked, and his eyes got real big, and I could see that he was salivating. He took two quick steps with Harmony in tow, and he was at the other side of the table. Harmony was on his left, and I wanted her to be on the right closer to me so I could grab her from him.

"Stop right there," I commanded. He stopped. "Now, give me Harmony, and you take the stones and leave." He released her arm, and she went behind him to come around the table toward me. As she got on the other side of him, he waited as she was almost around the table and grabbed her arm with his right hand and started to yank her back.

I had slid the bottle out of my back pocket and had it in my right hand behind my back, and in my left, I had quickly grabbed my pistol and was bringing them to the front of me as he grabbed her hand and yanked her back. I threw the water in his face and, at the same time, drew a bead on his face and pulled the trigger. The bullet hit him just below his right eye and passed through his skull and lodged in the chest of one of the other demons. At the same time, the water hit him, and he was gone.

Harmony was free, and I grabbed for her hand as one of the other demons threw himself at her to stop her. He hit the table where she had been standing, and I put a round in the back of his head. Harmony screamed and ran toward me.

Out of the corner of my eye, I saw Mica fly toward one of the other demons and grabbed him, yelling, "Run!"

I could not. I put Harmony behind me and turned toward the last demon and realized he was running the other way. I fired a shot in his direction, and he grabbed his leg but kept running. I fired again, and he fell but was still crawling away. I turned again toward the demon on the table and took my amulet and touched the back of his head, and he was gone. I walked down the hill toward the demon who was trying to crawl away and put another bullet in the back of his head and then touched his body with my amulet, and he was gone.

When I returned to Harmony, Mica was still fighting with the last demon, and they were rolling around on the ground. All of a sudden, Mica was on his feet and gave the demon a hard right to the jaw and then another. Every time the demon started to get his bearings, Mica would hit him again. Finally, the demon dropped on the ground and didn't move. I ran over to touch him, and as soon as I got close, he jumped up and grabbed me. I had one round left in the gun, so when he came around in front of me, I let him have it right in the chest, and he dropped to his knees. I quickly took my amulet and touched him, and he was gone.

I went over to the table and collapsed on the seat. Harmony came and sat beside me and hugged me. I was so proud of her for only screaming once, and I told her as much. She smiled and hit me on the arm. Mica came over and sat down at the table too. He was bleeding from a bite the demon made on his arm, but nothing severe. It all seemed to be a dream sometimes. I am nobody. Just like every person you would meet on the street. I don't have any powers. I am not superhuman, but here I am, fighting evil with what God gave me, a real great girlfriend and an angel. Okay, we do have an angel on our side. As we sat there in the middle of the night, I thanked my lucky stars that we were all not hurt.

We were just about four or five miles from my parents' house, so I suggested we drive to my parents and stay there for the night. Harmony could call her mom from there, and we could get some much-needed rest and something to eat. We all agreed that would be the best thing for us. The only problem was to tell my parents why Mica was with us and not to lie in the process. We decided to tell the truth. Mica is a friend of both Harmony and mine, so that was what we would tell them. We picked him up in Chicago, and he is coming home with us for a visit.

As we walked back to the car, I had to ask Mica one question; after all, he is an angel, and you don't get to talk to an angel all the time.

"Mica," I said. "In the Bible, man was made in God's image, and we are supposed to live forever. What happened that our life span came down to about one hundred years or so?"

I could see even in this light Mica was smiling at this question. "There was to be no sin until Adam and Eve ate the forbidden fruit," he replied. "After the first bite, both Adam and Eve's eyes were opened to sin, and the more sin in the world, the less life span man has. You eat the wrong things, drink the wrong things, listen, watch, and think the wrong things all your life, and yet you think the temple God gave you can endure all these things without any consequences to your mind, body, and soul?" Now it was my turn to smile.

We got to my parents' house about two thirty in the morning, and it took me several minutes to raise my mom to open the door to let us in. We talked for about ten minutes, then I showed Harmony the phone so she could call her parents. After that, we headed up to bed and sleep.

I showed Harmony to her bedroom, and she took me aside and closed the door. "David, when I talked to my mother, she told me one of the angels at the house went missing, and when they found him, he was badly beaten and had been bitten and clawed all over his body. The demons had done this to make him talk, so now they know we are coming back, and there will be no way to surprise them or sneak into town without them knowing."

"Well, we are still going to go through this, and we will pray we can survive and get the stones back without letting the demons have them," I said. I kissed her and went to my old room with Mica then went to bed. I have always known that a new day will make things seem better than the night before, but this day didn't seem any better as we ate breakfast and talked with my parents.

It was about 9:00 a.m. when we said goodbye and headed toward Missouri. Nobody said a word for several miles, and then we didn't say much until the last fifteen miles to home. Harmony relayed some more of her mother's conversation to us, and basically, she had said that the last mile to the house of Harmony's grandmother would be the worse, because after we cross the bridge, we will be safe and the demons cannot follow us from there to the house.

As we drove to the edge of town, I was thinking about what a pretty fall day it was. Fluffy clouds in the sky, leaves had turned yellow and orange and were all over the yards, and the temperature was about freezing. We were all looking and watching for signs of demons as we drove into town and by my house. Everything was okay as we got to the north side of town, and I turned onto the dirt road that ran along the river leading to the house of Harmony's grandmother, Maybell.

All of a sudden, from out of the cornfield along the river, a truck came up from behind us and hit us so hard it threw us over the bank and into the river. The hit was so hard it threw Mica right through the front windshield, and when I finally came to my senses, Mica's body was floating downstream facedown. I turned to Harmony, who was in the back seat, and grabbed her hand, pulling her to the front seat and out the door before the car started to sink.

The cold water revived Harmony, and she started gasping for air and swimming to the bank. I had to go back down in the water to the car and retrieve the bag of stones, and when I was in there, I felt the gun and grabbed it too. When I got to the surface, I was gasping for breath and saw Harmony standing on the bank shivering. I quickly swam to her and got out of the icy water too.

As I got my bearings, I realized we were on the wrong side of the river, and maybe that was a good thing because I could see three demons standing by the truck as we scrambled to the top of the bank and into the corn which had not been picked yet. It was a great place to hide.

Back home, when I was a young boy, we had cornfields and hayfields all around our house, and we would play hide-and-seek for hours in the corn in the summer and the fall. It was itchy in the summer, but in the fall, it would dry, and the only way you could follow someone was hearing them run rustling the stalks as their body hit them. If you were higher than the field, you could see the stalks move as the bodies moved through the cornfield. It was a great way to hunt deer in the fall.

Well, I didn't want anybody hunting me that way, so I told Harmony to stay low and not to touch the stalks of corn if she could help it.

I decided the best idea to get out of this would be to go away from Maybell's and head south to the nearest road, which would be about half of a mile. Then, we could cross the bridge back to town and start heading back north on the other side of the river. Hopefully, the demons would look for us north of the wreck, and we could sneak back to Harmony's grandmother's from behind them.

After about a quarter mile, we stopped and looked each over for cuts and any breaks. Harmony had a big cut on her left arm, and I had a big one on my face from the windshield, but we got the blood stopped, making a bandage from my shirt and keeping pressure on it until it stopped bleeding. I know her arm was hurting because my head was hurting terrible. I held her, and we talked about our plan.

"Harmony, I think we need to cross the river at the bridge and then make our way back north on the other side of the river. We could sneak past the demons if they are coming south on the east side of the river, and if they have crossed to the west, we are home free," I said.

"I think we need to walk to Mom's and get her car and drive most of the way back before we walk the rest of the way," she said.

"But, they will hear us and see us if we drive the car back there on the same road," I replied.

She agreed, and then we started back toward the bridge.

When we got to the road, we stepped out of the corn and hurried across the bridge to the east side. I had been on this road before, and there were several vacant houses along the river. It was eerie because I had went into some of them when Sam was alive. We went to one and stepped into the kitchen. The table was set, there was furniture in all the rooms and even clothes hanging in the closest, but nobody had lived there for years. It was as if they had just walked out the door and never returned. What had happened to the people who lived there?

As I was pondering that question, I heard a truck coming from around the corner from the north, and Harmony heard it too. We ran to the weeds and hid as the truck approached. When it got closer, I peeked out from the weeds just enough to see two demons driving it. We hunkered down and let the truck pass then got to our knees to watch it go down to the main road. When it got to the main road, it turned west toward the bridge we had just come across and stopped just as it got to the other side. Both demons got out and looked north into the corn we had just come through.

My heart was in my throat as we slipped away to the east and into the corn patch, where we headed north toward Maybell's house. I took Harmony's hand as we walked, and I could tell she was afraid as we walked. For some reason, the fear had left me when we entered the corn patch, and now hatred had taken its place. All the things these demons had done to me and my loved ones took its place in my heart. Both Harmony and Samantha had been hurt by these things, and Mica was gone too because of them. I just wanted to catch one by himself and beat the devil right out of him.

As we walked, I was trying to devise a plan to get by the demons and over the bridge, but nothing seemed to come to mind. We were about one hundred yards from the bridge when we got to the road that ran to the left and over the bridge. At the bridge, we could see four demons guarding it. According to Pearl, they could not cross onto the other side. I told Harmony to stop, and we got down on our knees to talk.

"What I suggest is that we split up here, and I will run across the road and see if I can get them to chase me into the corn. When they come after me, I want you to run as fast as you can over the bridge to freedom and safety. Then I will make a circle back to the bridge and cross to safety too."

"No," Harmony said. "We cross the road together run together, make the circle together, and then cross the bridge."

"Harmony?" I replied. "If I have to worry about your safety, I am afraid I cannot do what needs to be done. I love you and don't want them to take anything else away from me that I love. Please do as I ask, and when you are over the bridge, wait there for me."

I didn't let her answer that time. I kissed her on the mouth and looked into her beautiful brown eyes and told her I loved her and ran out into the road. The demons spotted me as I was running into the corn on the other side and were running toward me as I got into the corn. I could not look back to see if Harmony was running toward the bridge, but I was hopeful she was.

I heard the truck coming as I raced eastward away from the bridge but tried to listen for the rustle of the cornstalks to the left of me where the demons on foot were coming toward me. After about one hundred yards into the field, I turned north toward the bridge again and then, one hundred yards more, turned back south away from the bridge. I stopped when I was the farthest away from the bridge to listen if there was anything following me. I heard nothing, so I quietly started back toward the road and was hopeful they were looking farther east for me.

Just as I was about to get to the road, I heard the truck coming back from the bridge toward the south. It was coming right by me when they spotted me and made a turn into the corn and right back toward me. I was about 150 yards from the bridge and realized it was going to be a long shot to make it before they caught me with the truck, but I had no choice.

Out on the road, I ran and headed straight north to the bridge. I felt like the wind and my feet felt like they were not even touching the road as I ran. I had good wind in my lungs, and I felt like I could make it easy. The truck had made the turn into the road and was about fifty yards behind me from the sound of the engine. I knew I could make it then, so I just ran as fast as I could.

All of a sudden, out of the corn on the right came a big mean-looking demon right toward me. He was intending to tackle me as he got closer. His hands and arms were ready to grab me when I stopped and let him run right by me, and then I started running again. That made the truck get closer to me when I stopped, and the big one turned and came at me again. I was only fifteen yards from the bridge at this point, and I could see Harmony standing on the bridge with Maybell and Silvia yelling at the top of their lungs for me to run faster.

Then the truck caught up with me, and the passenger opened his door, and it hit me right in the back, then I went down head over heels to the ground. When I rolled over onto the ground, I tried to get my feet back under me to run again, but it was no use. One of the demons tackled me to the ground, and they all piled on. I was like a rag doll. Or more to the point, I felt like the straw man. I was thrown from one demon to the next, and they were doing their best to kill me.

I was beaten, scratched, kicked, bit, punched, thrown, and mauled to the point I was almost unconscious. And then all of a sudden, the killing was stopped. I could only see out of one eye, but there were two demons over me, and the rest were in a circle around them and me. The demons were fighting over me, I guess as to which one was going to finish me.

I rolled over on my stomach and started to crawl toward Harmony, who was yelling and crying at the same time. They must have come to an agreement, because all of a sudden, one grabbed me by the hair and stood me up and picked me up into his arms, still yelling in a language I had not heard before. When I was turned toward the one not holding me, it was Bellamy in front of me. I wanted to grab my amulet and stuff it down his throat, but I could see it was not hanging around my neck.

The one that held me kicked Bellamy away from me and turned toward all the other demons around us and raised me to the heavens, and I heard him say, "This is the prize, and I am taking the prize, so if there is one among you who thinks like Bellamy, please speak up, and I will show you who is boss."

Then he brought me down to face him, and that is when I saw it was Mica. He looked mean and evil and was twice the size he was when he was with us. He had fangs, and there was saliva dripping from them as he looked me right in my good eye and winked. We were just a few feet away from Harmony standing at the edge of the bridge.

Mica took the bag from my pocket and showed it to all the demons then passed it under the nose of Bellamy then, looking right at him, said, "Don't you know good always wins over evil?" then flipped the bag of stones back over his shoulder toward the bridge to Harmony.

When that happened, I hit the ground with a thud. They were gone; Mica and all the demons were gone in the blink of an eye. Harmony gave the bag to her grandmother and ran to help me. She kissed me, and then I passed out.

This is what I heard from Harmony about what happened next. They called the ambulance and told the sheriff I had been in an accident with my car going off the road into the river, which was true.

When they got me to the hospital, I had cuts, bruises, several broken bones; my spleen was ruptured, one eye out of the socket. Blisters had started growing in my mouth and down into my stomach, and I was in a coma from a severe head trauma.

The first thing they did was clean me up and try to stop all the bleeding. The doctor said it looked like a pack of wolves had ripped me apart. They could not keep the infection down, and nothing they tried seemed to kill it. They could not operate until they got the infection cleared up, so they just tried to keep me comfortable.

Harmony called my parents, and they came to see me several times, and she got a priest from her church to come and pray over me several times, but nothing seemed to help. Then one day, an old woman who came into the hospital for some tests came by the room and stopped. One of the nurses was there cleaning my wounds, and the older lady asked her what was wrong with me. The nurse said I had a bad infection, and they couldn't fight it with their medicines.

Harmony was there with me when the older lady came back in the evening. They talked, and she admired Harmony's amulet and how it shone when she was around me. Harmony told her that I was the love of her life and that several times I had saved her from certain death. The older woman left and then, an hour or so later, returned and told Harmony she wanted to help and took an amulet from around her neck and placed it around mine, then she kissed Harmony on the forehead and left.

Sometime in the evening, the night nurse was doing her rounds when she went into the older ladies' room. The nurse found only a burned spot on the chair where the woman had been sitting. There was just a burned blob of fat and some slippers on the floor just in front of the chair. Harmony later found out the older lady's name was Mary Beth Prall and she had lived in a small town between our town and the university.

The FBI came and questioned the night staff, the patients, Mary's family, and anybody who had contact with Mary since she came to the hospital. After two days, the FBI concluded it was Spontaneous Combustion that was the cause of the death and closed the books on the death. We knew better. Harmony and her family knew better; there was a "Rapture" right here in this small county hospital.

The next morning, after Mary's death, the doctor was making his rounds and came into my room. He checked the infection and thought it was starting to subside. It went on like that for about a week and was cleared up. The doctor operated setting bones and taking out my spleen. They said that when I woke, they would check my sight on the bad eye.

Oh, I had both shoulders dislocated, and one of my hips was also dislocated. They relocated them and put me in a sling for both arms and a brace to hold my hip in place until it strengthened. It was strange that the doctor never said a word the whole time I was in the hospital about the numerous bite marks all over my body. Everything could be explained by the car crashing off the hillside into the river except the bites.

I awoke on the fourth month and was starving. Then I went back to sleep for a good eight hours, until Harmony and my family came to see me. I was tired but was happy that I was alive and able to see my family once again.

Another month, and I went home to Pearl's house, where everybody took real good care of me, especially the fallen angels. They were always helping me to shave, eat, bathe me, dress me—anything needed to be done, they helped. I still didn't understand a word they were saying, but I could see the love they had for me, and I was thankful.

When I could get out and walk again, it was the end of April. I had to walk with a cane and sometimes help from Harmony. She was always by my side when she was not at class in the university. I am so proud of her. We would take a walk downtown and back, then the next day, one more block and back. Soon I was walking all the way back home to the house I had bought Sam.

When I walked by myself, I would sit on the porch of my old house and just watch the birds and squirrels play around the trees. All I wanted to do is take it easy and get stronger so I could go back to work.

One Saturday, Harmony took me for a checkup at the hospital, and that is where she told me she wanted to be a doctor. I could not be more pleased, and I told her so. The doctor gave me a clean bill of health to go back to work, but half day to start. I was elated about the news.

I moved back home, and Harmony moved with me. I would work in the morning, and in the afternoon, I would walk and lift weights, waiting for her to come home. Tuesdays and Thursdays were the best days because she got out of school when I got off work at noon. Those days we spent out at her grandmother's helping around the house and the grounds. We planted a big garden and spent many hours tending it.

In June, after Harmony got out of school for the summer, we got married. It was decided we should live with Harmony's grandmother and aunt, and we were happy to do it. I loved the house, the grounds, and the river that ran behind the house. Harmony and I both felt at ease here. The other nice thing was, right after the stones had been given to Maybell, the sun shone on the house every day after, even if it was raining, snowing, or the rest of the area was under clouds.

Harmony and I decided to fix up my old house and rent it out so we could have some extra money. The first thing was, we were going through the house to make a list of things that needed attention. We came to the back room with all the handprints on the wall. I wanted to save as much of the walls to relocate it somewhere in our new home.

"Harmony, how could we save these prints from the wall without taking the whole wall?" I asked.

I could see that an idea had just come to her when she said, "That is it. I know what is missing in this room. There was a built in bookshelf on that east wall when I came to see my grandmother. She has covered it up."

"Who has covered it up?" I asked.

"My grandmother covered it up years ago when I was two or three before she moved to the farm. I remember playing on the floor when my mother and her were wallpapering that area. And I know how to preserve your prints. We can carefully steam the wallpaper off the walls and take the paper and put it on a wall in our house." Her grandmother had given us the east side of the house to do as we wished with.

We were so excited we got into the car and drove the fifteen miles to the rent-a-center to see if they had a steamer. They did, and we rented it for the weekend and hurried back to the house with it.

We steamed all the paper off the walls on the west side of the room, and it worked great. Next we went to the east side where Harmony's grandmother had put paper over the built-in bookshelf. As we were working with the steamer in this area, we both noticed it was not working as well. We got the major part of the wallpaper off, but there was one spot that would not come off, and I was getting madder every second. Finally, I blew up, which is not my way, and hit the wall with my fist. I punched a hole the size of my fist in the wall. After all, it was just Sheetrock.

Harmony grabbed me, and we both set down on the floor so I could cool off. As we were sitting there, a single gold coin fell out of the hole and rolled right to our feet. Harmony picked it up and looked at it and gave it to me, and I looked at it too.

We were both on our feet in a second, me with my fist and Harmony with a hammer ripping big chunks of sheet rock off the wall. The coins started coming out of the holes we made and didn't stop coming until we had more than a thousand gold twenty-dollar gold pieces at our feet strewn between the ripped-up Sheetrock. We were both exhausted and fell to the floor, both of us picking up the gold and stacking it in a pile between us.

Harmony talked first, saying, "You know we can't keep this gold, it is my grandmother's."

I shook my head in agreement and said, "Let's put it in a box and take it to her and show her what we found." We did just that. We found an old wooden box in the shed and put all the gold in it and drove it back to the farm.

When we got inside the house, we found both ladies sitting out on the back porch, drinking iced tea, and talking. We put the box on the table so both women could see what was in it, and we sat down with Harmony on my lap. The ladies both looked in the box and smiled, and then they both turned and looked at us.

Maybell said, "Well, what do we have here?" with a grin on her face.

Harmony answered, "You know what it is, Grandmother, and where it came from."

Maybell looked at Silvia and said, "I don't know what you are talking about," with another grin. Then her eyes shifted to me and then back to Harmony. "Harmony, my dear child, this money is for you and your husband. It is not mine. I was just saving it for you and him until you were old enough to have it. It was given to me by an angel for deeds not yet done. The deed is done, and it is yours and your husband's to do what you want with it." Then she and Silvia took their glasses and went inside the house without another word.

We were both sitting there with not a word to say about the situation. After I had found my composure, I said to Harmony, "What are we going to do with all this money?"

She looked at me and said, "Well, my idea is to take some of it and build onto this house so all of us can live here. Mother, Father, Granny, Silvia, and all the fallen angels. I want us all to be under one roof." Then she turned to me and gave me a great big kiss. I smiled, and I was in agreement. Life is too short not to have family and friends close. So that very day, we made a plan to start building on to the house to accommodate everyone, after we had talked it over with Pearl and Mia.

The first thing was to sell some of the gold to get enough money to buy the material. It was decided I should quit my job and I would be the carpenter and general manager for the project. We ran an ad in the local paper and got quite a responses for someone to buy the gold. Gold was about $300 an ounce, but with the added value of the coins, we got more. We just sold what we needed to buy all the supplies to build the addition. I say "addition," but it ended up being just as big as the original house and then some.

I needed help, so we took out another ad for a master carpenter. We had several apply, and we settled on an older gentleman with plenty experience. He was great and worked well with me. We didn't get done until the next spring, and I was happy but was sad to let my help go. Sometimes I would call him if I had a project, and he would come and help.

Harmony got pregnant, and we decided I would stay at home with our child, and she would finish her schooling. We had two children, Martin Lenard Hunter and Faith Ann Hunter. They are grown now and have families of their own.

I am basically retired, although I am just over sixty years old.

Harmony is the administrator of the hospital now.

There are just two more things I would like to add to this story— one being if you are as smart as I think you are, go online and check out what I have been telling you about Rapture and Spontaneous Combustion.

Two, I told you I would tell you where I live. There is a river that runs on the west side of Missouri called the Nodaway River. About forty miles south of the Iowa-Missouri border, there is a university. If you follow the river north about fifteen miles, you will come to an old river town, and north of it about a mile, you will see a big white sprawling home on a hilltop on the right riverbank. There is a white staircase leading up to the house from the river. Tie up your boat and come up the stairs, and I will make us some tea.

ABOUT THE AUTHOR

Douglas was born in a little town, Lamoni, Iowa, where he grew up and attended public school, graduating in 1971. Douglas attended Graceland University in Lamoni, Iowa, Northwest Missouri University in Maryville, Missouri, and graduated at Graceland University in 1988 with a BA in business education.

Douglas used his degree to help people by managing several private group homes for troubled youth, which also housed shelter wings that held youth for the courts. Later he worked with mental disabled adults in independent living housing. He has owned and operated several businesses through the years and still owns several businesses in Texas.

Along the way, he raised a family in his hometown and now lives in Texas with his wife.

Douglas says that without the help and support of family and friends, this book would not have been possible.